Thanks to my proofing team:

> Katherine Anderson-Davilla
> Brendan LaSalle
> Mike Morrey

> You guys are the best!

Published by Pandahead Publishing, a division of Pandahead Productions. Pandahead Publishing and the pandahead logo are trademark of Pandahead Productions.

Book design by Pandahead Productions

Cover design and illustration by Dave Johnson

Please visit www.publishing.pandahead.com

Print ISBN: 978-1-944209-00-1
Ebook ISBN: 978-1-944209-01-8

DEDICATION

A special shout-out to Bobby Politte, who had a conversation with me one night about why zombies always just wanted to eat people.

Big thanks to Dave Johnson for producing such an amazing cover, and being an even more amazing person.

And a deepfelt dedication to my incredible wife, Allyson. Your love and support keeps me going.

-Brett Brooks

EDIBLE COMPLEX

BY
BRETT
BROOKS

Chapter One

So, the zombie apocalypse happened.

Nobody is really sure how or why it happened, but everyone knows where the end of the world began. Minneapolis, Minnesota. The city that can send a chill down your spine in so many ways.

It would be ridiculous to think that anyone saw this coming, so when it happened we were all a little taken aback. I mean, you read about these things, but you never think that it is going to happen to you. Or at all, actually. One thing that kept with popular thinking was the speed of it, though. The first reports of the zombies came on a Thursday morning. By Saturday night it had covered most of the state, and then by the following Saturday everywhere in North America was having to deal with the issue.

Now, I should be clear on a couple of things, I suppose. First off, by zombie "apocalypse" I really mean the fact that zombies are pretty much everywhere now. And I might have exaggerated slightly with the "end of the world" comment, too. What I mean is that you can't go anywhere without seeing dozens or more of them wandering about. On the good news side is the fact that they aren't constantly trying to kill all the living. And yes, the key word in that sentence is "constantly."

Oh, and it's not like a lot of the movies or books we used to read about the subject where someone would get bitten and then a few hours later be frothing at the mouth and mumbling about brains and shambling around. What actually happens if you get bitten by a zombie is that it hurts. No more or less than a really hard bite from any other person that might get the urge to do it, though. No, not like that little love nip you might get on a particularly frisky night in bed, but like you were sitting in front of your favorite meal and going to town. Teeth into flesh type painful, in other words.

The only exception to that rule, of course, is if the zombie actually overpowers the person and they die from severe trauma brought on by excessive hunger. Which you could also just call being eaten alive. If that happens, then whatever is left—if there is enough left—will pop up a few hours later as a zombie of its own. But then again, if you die from a car crash you become a zombie. From heart attack? Zombie. Death duel with an ex lover? Zombie. Forgetting to properly pack your parachute? Really messy zombie.

So, no bite transferable disease here. Just dead people coming back to life. Which really isn't much better, actually.

The point is that it isn't the zombies that are creating the zombies. It's death that is creating the zombies, and for the life of us—no pun intended—we can't figure out why. If any human dies, they are going to come back as a zombie a few hours later. Thankfully, thus far it has only been the humans who are coming back, too. I would hate to have to deal with dead animals of every type showing back up. Or insects. That would be downright creepy, really.

It's hard enough feeding the human zombies, after all.

Which reminds me: we're feeding them. The zombies, I mean. All day, all night, every day we are feeding the zombies. All they want to do is eat it seems, and they are very picky about what makes them hungry. Actually, you know, that's not exactly true. They aren't picky, they are exclusive eaters. By that I mean all they will eat is one thing. Remember the whole "braaaaiinssss" thing? Well, substitute whatever the current food of choice is among them, and you have the right idea. And you damn well better have their next meal ready, or they are going to pitch a bit of a fit—which usually results in massive amounts of damage and sometimes a little death.

Currently, it's cabbage. The local meal of choice, I mean. Green cabbage to be precise, but we've noticed that we can mix in other types of cabbage with it and they will let it slide. It is kind of amusing to hear them moan "caaaabaaaaggge" though, which is about the only perk. I hear it's sauerkraut in Alabama, which sounds particularly aromatic if you ask me, and not in a good way. Oh yeah, it's not a universal food the zombies want, either. Local tastes and all that, I guess.

So anyway, around the clock right now we are growing and picking and processing cabbage, trying to get it into the hands of the zombies as fast as possible. Which, considering it takes up to six months to grow a head, makes the idea of fast completely relative. Most estimates have us looking at about three weeks until we run out, which leads us to the seemingly never ending question: what then?

We never know what the damn things are going to want to eat. Before cabbage it was eggs. Before eggs it was refined sugar. Before that was…peanut butter? I honestly don't remember. That's kind of sad, really.

The egg time was pretty good, since getting eggs is a lot easier than getting cabbage, at least from a number viewpoint, but, like always, there was a lull, and that seems to be all it takes.

Soon enough, the cabbage will be gone, they'll throw a fit, and then move on to the next thing, whatever it might be.

There are teams of scientists working on that little question constantly. Trying to figure out what the next flavor is going to be. And every time they come up with a new theory to test, it immediately gets shot to hell. They used to come out and tell us their theories all the time, but now they just keep to themselves and don't say much. You can't really blame them, though, after eight years of trying and failing, most of the world just doesn't want to hear another premise that is going to go nowhere.

The one idea—the one fear—that we all live in is that they are going to go the route of the movies. That the next thing on their menu is going to be us. So far, we've been lucky—for the most part. There was a reported incident of it happening in the Appalachian Mountains, but everyone sort of wrote that off as normal behavior for the area. Eventually, though, it's gonna happen. We're going to run out of the food du jour, and then they are going to look up and see their next meal as the folks that have been feeding them.

Scientists are also desperately trying to figure out not only how this whole thing started, but also how it can be stopped or reversed. They've had less luck at that than they have with the food issue—at least as far was we can tell. They haven't made any announcements at all about it. We all hope for this one, but we've also learned to temper our hope.

And I'm sure that some of you—at least the violent types—are wondering why the military doesn't just come in and wipe all these damn things off the globe in a massive show of force and spectacle that is sure to please the general movie-going public. Well, they tried. Several times, in fact. The problem with trying to get rid of the dead by killing them is pretty self-explanatory though, when you think about it. That whole shoot-them-in-the-head thing doesn't work. It just creates a hungry zombie with a hole in its head. And let me tell you, there are few things less pleasant than dealing with than a zombie that has a bit of brain leaking out. Some folks wanted to burn them, but burning a body to ash is a lot tougher than most people think, and just the idea of a flaming zombie walking towards me is enough to make me pucker. Though, thinking on it, Flaming Zombie would be a good name for a drink or a band.

Anyway, there is also the small matter of them fighting back. If you have a well fed zombie, it tends to just mill about until it has the urge to eat again. If you're lucky, that means that you've got about six or seven hours, but times vary based on the size and nature of the zombie itself. But an angry zombie, a zombie that you have decided to attack, well, it defends itself. And one zombie getting angry tends to translate over to the next, and then the next, and then…. Well, you get the picture. The massive, blood-soaked, more-zombie-creating picture.

Oh, we did try to contain them, too. Put them in a big area out in the middle of nowhere with a giant fence around it, but that didn't work, either. They stayed put for a while, but when you get that many zombies together they tend to get on each other's nerves—or whatever the zombie equivalent of nerves might be—and it leads to agitation, which leads to violence, which leads to broken fences and rioting zombies, and we're back to the this-is-a-bad-idea place.

So, we're feeding them. And right now, in these parts at least, we are feeding them cabbage. Or at least, to clarify, the Northeast Atlanta Federal Office of Organizing Dining for Zombies—or F.O.O.D.Z. as the people-who-decide-to-name-these-places-so-they-can-have-a-crappy-anagram call it—is feeding them cabbage. And metro Atlanta isn't the ideal area to grow cabbage, either. It's too warm most of the time. Which means that the majority of our cabbage is trucked in from other states.

Yes, the other states and the lines of communication and all of that are still up and intact, but a few things have certainly changed. For one, living conditions have gone down the crapper in general. Money isn't as important in this day and age, since we're all in the same industry now: zombie herding and feeding—which makes the former execs a little upset, actually. Oh, we still have our own needs for food and shelter, but a lot of the more extravagant things—like bowling or golf or reality television—are gone. Some of this is an obvious improvement.

In fact, I'm one of those who lost my old job. I used to work as the promotions manager for a travel agency. That sort of falls into the whole extravagant category, so it didn't last too long in a post-zombies-exist world. Now I work as one of the distribution managers at the aforementioned F.O.O.D.Z. location, working about sixty hours a week and still trying to find time to not just stay alive, but to actually live. And in this time, that's a much more difficult task than almost anything else. I'll get to that in a bit, though.

That's hardly everything, of course. It's just the tip of the iceberg, so to speak. I'll get to as much as I can as we move along, which I suppose we should do. There are a lot of things that have to be said before my story is done.

Me? Oh, well, my name is Cassandra Cole—though most folks call me Cici—and I guess you could say that this is the story of my life, such as it is.

Which is better than the story of my death, I suppose, which thankfully, this isn't.

Chapter Two

"Morning!" I know how he's going to answer even before my greeting has left my mouth.

"Every day around this time," he mumbles. Okay, I got the words right, but I wasn't expecting the mumble, but then again it is his job to keep an eye out on hundreds of zombies gathered together to get themselves a head of cabbage. Which, unfortunately, is also my job.

"Something bothering you, Dave?"

"I dunno."

I like Dave, I really do, but sometimes—like these times, actually—he challenges that idea. I mean, it's perfectly obvious that something is bugging him, and he wears it on his sleeve, but for whatever reason he would rather it just be a big annoyance to everyone around him rather than share it. So, it's time to begin the little dance we share.

"Seems like something is bothering you." Stepping up beside him, I stare out in the same general direction as him. The feeding dock is completely open air, so it looks out over what we call The Table—the area where the zombies get fed—which is basically a large fence funneling them in one direction and ushering them out another after they pick up their food.

"Nah, I'm fine."

It's just after dawn, and the light has that odd tint to it, sort of yellow but with a not-really-red along with a hint of blue. Which means that it should be mud brown, actually. And the air feels damp and unsettled, which just makes me fidgit. Do you get that feeling, too? I dunno, maybe everyone sees the morning differently, depending on their personal preference. I've never been a morning person—I'm more of a night owl— so it's always felt just off to me. Like it still needs to finish cooking or something. The odd part is that Dave is a morning person. He works overnight, and I work day shift. We've tried switching shifts but even in a post-zombie-apocalyptic world it seems nearly impossible to get a corporate boss to change their minds.

"Okay." I nod and keep what I'm sure looks like a fake smile on my face. "Well, what's our status? Did you have any issues last night?"

"Nah. Not really." He takes a deep breath and turns towards me. Normally, I would call Dave plain-looking. Not a bad looking guy, mind you, just...plain. If he took some time he might actually be able to make himself fairly attractive. Dark hair. Grey eyes. Sure, he could stand to lose a little weight, but he's not that bad off. Attitude goes a long way, though, and that scowl on his face just doesn't do anything to help his looks, so he's dropped just below plain at the moment.

"Good. Hopefully it'll be a smooth day, too," I tell him in complete honesty. The days where I have to do nothing but oversee the job are the best ones. Gets me out of here on time and I get to go home and—

"Well, there was one thing."

Crap. He couldn't even let me suggest having a relaxing night after work, could he? I sigh without even realizing it.

"What was it?" I ask.

He turns back to look out at The Table again. "It's just…" He takes a deep breath, and exhales it quickly. "Do they seem to be moving slower to you?"

Now, contrary to popular fiction, zombies aren't slow shambling monsters, but they aren't exactly fast-paced, either. They basically act like someone with no place to be, and just meander from spot to spot at a steady pace. Think about a stoner on a beach just strolling around looking for a snack. That's what these things are like—almost exactly, actually. Anyway, when they're at The Table they tend to move a little slower because—as odd as this sounds—they generally have no issue with standing in line and waiting their turn.

"Um, not really," I answer honestly. "No slower than normal, anyway."

"Yeah. Yeah, it's probably just me." He nods. I wait, because I know he isn't done talking. "Still, don't they look a little slower to you?"

"Dave, I've only been here about ten minutes. Right now the zombies look like zombies." I shrug. "Sorry."

"Yeah, you're right. Ignore me." He turns away and I go with him. We've got about an hour overlap in our time here to go over everything before he gets to head home and I get to take over. And let me tell you, it is such exciting information. I'm sure it's important, but ultimately it seems like bureaucracy in action to me. In fact, it's so exciting, let's skip that bit and consider about an hour to have passed.

"Have a nice day, Dave!" I wave as he heads towards the exit.

He waves back without saying a word and I turn to go about my business.

I move over to the head of The Table, looking out at the zombies lined up—well, more corralled up, I suppose—for their regular feeding. Hundreds of creatures in various states of decay hoping to not completely decompose before they get their cabbage.

Without even thinking about it I shake my head. It's hard not to feel sorry for these things. They don't speak beyond the occasional droning word. They don't laugh at all. They don't seem to do much save for go from one event like this to the next, always looking for their fix. I want there to be something more to them. Something more for them. For them to have a social life and exist beyond this small patch of land, but all I can do is watch them wander in and out of The Table and disappear for a few hours afterward.

The guys at the dock are switching out. One of my duties is to make sure that there are the right number of people handling the situation. According to F.O.O.D.Z. guidelines, a facility using a feeding dock of our size is supposed to always have a minimum of nine employees, and a maximum of twelve, handling the food distribution at what we affectionately call The Mouth—basically the exact change point of The Table. This keeps the flow going regularly and doesn't get the food out too quickly or too slow.

That's right, we've discovered that you can feed the zombies too quickly. Strange as it may sound, if you give them too much, too quickly they start to discard the food before they've finished it, and want the new one while the old one wastes away. So we have a pace and tempo to keep at, which is another of my duties, actually. I make sure that the food goes out in a steady flow.

Most of my duties can be summed up with the following statement: I watch things. I watch the crew do their job and make sure that nothing is screwed up. I watch the flow of the food to make sure that it is going out at the right pace. I watch to make sure that the stocking team is getting the supply to the dock so that the delivery crew doesn't run out of food. It's just management. I make sure that all of the parts are running smoothly without getting in the way. If something goes wrong, then it's my job to step in and make sure that it gets fixed.

Luckily, the worst thing that has happened is that I had one day where three guys were out with the flu and two others were struggling with it. That meant I had to move some people around, lend a personal hand, and call in emergency replacements, but that's about it. Mostly, I just watch what goes on.

Which takes us to about two or so hours after I got to work that day.

He is standing off to the side. Just standing there, by himself. He is a fairly tall, male zombie, who looked to have curly brown hair back when he was alive. He has already gone through the queue at The Table, gotten himself a big head of green cabbage, and then he just stopped. He stands there holding the cabbage in front of him. Occasionally he raises it up above his head slightly, but that is about it. He isn't eating a single bite of it, but just holding it. Like a precious gem on display for all around him to see and admire.

If it just lasted a few minutes I probably wouldn't have thought twice about it, but he stands there holding that cabbage for over four hours. Other zombies walk by from time to time, and I swear that he raises his vegetable treasure up above him each time another one gets close. At first I think it's to keep it out of their hands so they don't steal his dinner, but the longer it goes on the less that seems reasonable.

I get the feeling he is showing it off.

To whom? And why? It's not like every other zombie walking past him doesn't have the exact same thing in their hands—or a very close variation of it, at least. So why that cabbage? And why show it off? And what the heck is a zombie doing wanting to show off anything, anyway?

Apparently I am a little fixated on this one zombie, too. To the point where others noticed.

"Cici?"

I turn around to find Juan Phillips, our shipping manager, standing behind me. I quickly pull myself together and give him a reply. "Hey. What's up? You need help with something?"

"No, not really. I was just checking in with the guys at The Mouth and saw you here. You look a little out of it. You feeling okay?" His eyes squint at me in that expression somewhere between confusion and concern.

"Yeah, I'm fine. Just got distracted." I give him a big reassuring smile. "Daydreaming about a better life, I suppose. Flow going okay?" Business talk. It's a good way to distract from what is probably me being crazy, which I don't want to bring to the attention of a co-worker.

"A little off, actually. We're going through less cabbage than expected. Which is good, I suppose, since that means it'll give us plenty of time to get levels right." Juan glances down at his ever-present clipboard. I'm reasonably sure he schedules out his bathroom breaks on that thing, but I've never had the courage to check. I stifle a bit of a giggle at my own joke—at least until his words sink in.

"Did you just say that things are going slower?" I raise an eyebrow.

"A little bit." He nods and raises up the top page on his clipboard, looking at something related to the rate of our feeding schedule, I suppose. "Nothing drastic, but enough that it's going to give us a bit of surplus on the day."

"Really? Huh." I have this tendency to hold my mouth slightly open and feel the edge of my teeth with my tongue while I'm thinking sometimes. From the look in Juan's eyes, I'm doing it right now. I close my mouth into a big smile. "Well, gotta give Dave some credit, then. He said he thought our dinner guests were moving a little slower last night."

"Good eye," Juan says with an approving nod. "I'll leave a note for him to stop by and see me tomorrow to see if things mesh up. Maybe he's spotted something."

"Yeah, could be. Anything to keep the zombies happy, right?" I mean that, too.

"Oh yeah!" His eyes light up in agreement. "All right, well, I guess I'll let you get back to work. Talk to you later." He raises two fingers up off his clipboard in a semblance of a wave. I lift my right hand halfway to acknowledge him.

As soon as he is far enough away that all of his attention is on whatever comes next, I turn back to find my proud zombie and his prize cabbage. He's gone. I look around just trying to pick him up in the crowd, but I can't locate him at all.

Whatever he was doing, he's done with it now. And he did help to kill four hours of my day, which means that I'm in the home stretch before I get to get out of here and go try to have some actual fun tonight.

Lucky me.

Chapter Three

Dating these days is pretty hit or miss. I mean, with the threat of the end of the world hanging over us every day the concept of long-term relationships has pretty much flown out the window. Everyone seems to be living for the now instead of the future. Nobody wants that burden. So, we screw around a lot, both figuratively and literally. And it's all for fun. We just want to have a good time to take our minds off what might be waiting around any corner.

I wish I could say I was different, but…well, there was a reason why I showed up at the club tonight. And it wasn't just to meet up with Julie.

They say there is an exception to every rule, and Julie Newmark is a walking example to prove it. In a world where we are all too scared to do anything but pick up the latest distraction, Julie reminds us that there used to be something more. That sometimes the greatest display of courage possible is just to live your life normally.

Julie is my best friend. Easily my best friend. I would go so far as to say that everyone else in my life right now is barely more than an acquaintance, but Julie is a dyed-in-the-wool friend. The type that is going to take your side, even if she knows that you're wrong—and then bitch to you about it later in private. Basically, the best kind of best friend.

I've only known her for a little over three years. She used to work at a coffee shop I went to on a regular basis and we would talk every day when I stopped by on my way to work and eventually we just started talking outside of her job. Despite knowing her that little amount of time, I've never known anyone with whom I've felt so close. She just gets me.

Our normal hangout is Tatters. I wouldn't go so far as to call it a dive bar, but it's certainly not an upper echelon kind of place. I mean, it's nice, I guess. In a way. Sort of. They try to be nicer than they have the budget for, I think. They serve food—bar food, but decent bar food—and they have a drink menu that includes all manner of fruity drinks meant to attract women to the place. It works, I guess, since Julie and I have been coming here since we started hanging out together—and Julie longer than that. It's where she met her husband, actually, back before everything went to hell.

As I hit the door I look towards our normal table—which is more to say the area of the bar where we always try to get a table. True enough, I see her sitting in a booth, her head casually bobbing side-to-side along with the music that is almost, but not quite, too loud to carry on a conversation.

She sees me coming and her head pops up brightly, and I can't help but smile. If nothing else, being around Julie is enough to make sure that my day gets better. I'm not sure it's possible for her to be in a truly bad mood.

"Hey, girlfriend!" she says in a little sing-song voice and pats the table in front of her. "How was your day?" I think about an answer, but never get a chance to say it. "Today was a great day. Ask me why today was a great day."

I slide into the booth and glance over to see if the waitress catches my arrival. A quick nod from her is enough to verify, and I turn my attention back across the booth. "Sure, I'll play along. Why was today a great day, Julie?" I look at her with exaggerated, though not fake, interest.

"Mike got his promotion! Yay!" She claps her hands and bounces a little bit.

"All right!" My face lights up a little. Actually, that is great news. Julie's husband, Mike, has been working on getting that promotion for over a year now. He is a cop with the Cobb County Police Department—the suburb I live in north of Atlanta—and he has spent most of the past few years on perimeter patrol, making sure that the zombies stayed out of the heavily populated areas and, oh, "gently" escorting any stragglers back out into the outlying areas. Not the safest of jobs, as sometimes zombies just don't want to be forcefully moved, but severe injury was very rare. Very rare doesn't mean never, though, and a few cops have lost their lives just trying to make sure that people are safe. "Shouldn't you go and be with him? Celebrate?"

"He's working, but we're going to celebrate later." She nods quickly. "Well, as much as we can." She pats her stomach gently and grins.

That's the other thing about Julie: she's pregnant. Not something you see a lot of in the world today. It seems there is a pessimistic view about bringing new life into a world where the dead have risen up. Go figure. Julie, though, she keeps right on plugging away. And she and Mike have their first child on the way. She's not showing yet, but that's likely to change soon. She's about ten weeks in, so we're expecting a bump any time now.

"Hey, you tear that club soda up!" I chuckle. "Just let him have his fun."

"Oh, don't worry, he's gonna be having fun," she says with a smile. I immediately try to get the image of a fetus dodging a missile out of my head.

"So, have you guys thought about things past tonight? What you're going to do?" I cock my head suddenly wondering something. "It does have a pay raise, right? This isn't just a change in title and responsibility, is it?"

"Slight pay raise, but to be honest, we wouldn't care about the money. We just want him to be closer in. Safer," she says in a very matter-of-fact manner.

"No big plans, then? Just happy with a little extra cushion each month?"

"Uh-huh!" She nods repeatedly in a quick, sharp motion.

Out of the corner of my eye I spot the waitress making it up to the table. She's been working here for a while, but I hate to say that I don't know her name. It could be Mary or Margaret or some other "M" name—I think. I'm horrible with names unless they are driven into my head repeatedly.

"How are you gals tonight?" Her voice has that chipper edge to it. The one that you can never be sure is real or extremely practiced.

"She's great," I motion to Julie, "and I'm hoping to feel the same way in an hour or so."

The response I get is definitely a practiced laugh. "Well, what can I bring you to help get that started?"

"Whiskey tonic, please."

"You want a lime in that, sweetie?" Ah, that's right. She's one of those women. The "sweetie," "honey," "darlin'" type.

"That sounds great. Thanks." I smile up at her.

She turns to Julie. "You doin' okay, hon?"

Straw in mouth, Julie simply moves her eyes and nods a little. It's enough to send the waitress off on her epic quest to get my drink. At least that's what I like to think she's doing.

"So, how was work?" Julie asks as she moves away from her straw.

I shrug. "It was work. Watched a lot of zombies eat. Felt grateful that the breeze was blowing out away from The Table."

"Stench is that bad, huh?" She wrinkles up her nose.

"I can't believe that you still haven't been close enough to smell one." If it was at all possible in this day and age, Julie would be the person I would list as having a sheltered life.

"Why would I?" Her upper body shivers. "Those things are disgusting. And scary. And dangerous! I'm happy that I've never smelled one before."

"You know, you can get close to them. If they're fed they are fairly harmless so long as you don't aggravate them. I'm close to them all the time." It's true. Been arm's length away more times than I can count. Granted it's been with a railing between us all but two times, but still….

"Well, forgive me for not wanting to be near an undead creature. Those things are not natural, Cici! Don't start thinking otherwise! You're too close to it to see how bad they really are." Her words are deeply impassioned, and I try to tell myself that she's wrong.

Thankfully, the waitress arrives at the table, giving me a good excuse to not debate her on the matter.

"Here you go, sweetie." She sets a napkin down on the table, quickly followed by a drink. "And just to let you know, it's compliments of the gentleman at the bar." Her eyes glance sideways, providing a rough direction for me to follow. I do just that, and Julie does the same—albeit a little more obviously as she leans forward and twists sideways.

There are a good half dozen guys sitting at the bar, three of which happen to be looking our way. Thankfully, one of them raises his glass as he sees me look over. I take that as a sign, and raise the glass back at him with a nod.

"Cute," Julie says with a nudge behind her voice.

"Not bad." Okay, he is kind of cute, really. He has that whole tall, dark, and handsome thing going for him. No, that's a thing, really.

"He's coming this way," Julie turns and straightens herself up, runs her fingers through her hair and her tongue over her lips once, seemingly trying to look pretty for him. And dammit, I'm doing the same thing. He's at the table before we know it.

"Hi." Great. He has a deep, smooth voice, too. I'm doomed. "My name's Terry."

"Thanks for the drink." I raise it up as evidence that he actually did provide the drink in question.

"You're welcome." He glances over at Julie, but only for a moment, and then he's back looking at me. And I'm eating that up, actually. "What's your name? If you don't mind me asking?"

"I'm Julie. She's Cici." That was so nice of my friend to answer for me. I smile anyway.

"Nice to meet you two." He glances at the booth. "Are you ladies alone tonight?"

"Yeah!" And with that response I openly glare at Julie. Her face twists a little as she speaks to me, "What?"

"If I'm bothering you, I can just…" Terry takes a half step backwards, using his thumb to point back to the barstool from whence he came.

"No, it's fine," I quickly answer, but still manage a dirty look at Julie. "Hold on, let me just…" I pop up and move over to sit beside Julie, carefully nudging her over with my hip. With a little show I point to my now-empty side of the booth. "There. Have a seat."

"Thank you. So, how's your night going?" Aw dammit. He smiled. His smile is as pretty as the rest of him.

"Pretty." Use more words, Cici. Add more words to that right now. "Good. Pretty good. How are you?"

Yeah, that's the kind of sweet talk that draws guys in like flies.

"Things are going much better now."

That was such a cheesy line. Which makes the fact that I laughed at it just that much worse.

"I take it they were going badly before?" I play along. Why not?

"Not too bad, actually, it's just better now." Okay, that's not going anywhere. Time to change tactics.

"What were you doing earlier?" I ask and then take a sip of my drink. The slight burn hits the back of my throat and warms me all the way down.

"Working. Just trying to make progress and getting kinda nowhere." He half rolls his eyes. Brown eyes. Dreamy, deep, rich brown eyes. "Nothing to worry about, though."

"Where do you work?" Julie pipes in.

"The CZC," he announces casually.

Woah. That's serious. The Center for Zombie Control is the leading research facility in the country. Just about every major issue stemming from the zombie situation runs through that building. It's where every person committed to finding a solution to the apocalypse wants to be, and the place that everyone hopes is going to give the press conference we all dream about. It's like a dream castle of zombie research. They've even walled off the center since the whole thing began, just to be safe. If you drive around just east of downtown, and you happen to see something that looks like a giant fortress, you've probably found the right building.

"Wow! Cici works with zombies, too!" Julie's head bobs towards me in a short jerky motion.

"Uh, not quite the same way," I explain. "I basically just work as an area supervisor at a feeding station. Nothing like what you do."

"Well, actually, it's kinda the same," he laughs and, dammit, he's got a cute laugh, too. "My job is to…" He winces. "Actually, I'm not allowed to say what my job is. Sorry. But, it's really not too different. So, you work with F.O.O.D.Z., then?"

I nod quickly after another sip and set my glass down. "Yeah, another cog in the feeding machine." A thought runs through my head. "Wait, the CZC is over east of town, isn't it? What are you doing this far north?"

"I live up here, actually. Pretty close by to here." He nods and takes a drink of his beer. The foam sits on his upper lip just long enough for his tongue to come out and clean it away. He smacks his lips a couple of times and then gives me that same damn smile.

And I feel something flutter inside.

No, Cici. Do not say it. This way, way too fast. Don't be that girl. Just smile or something. It's okay.

The words are already coming out of my mouth, aren't they?

"How close by?"

Chapter Four

Not that I'm complaining. Quite the opposite, actually. It was great. He was great. Is great. Whatever tense would be best to use, I suppose. I guess past tense though, since he's sleeping now and I'm not. I'm not even slightly tired, honestly.

Ah, the joys of being a night owl.

Could be worse, though. At least he doesn't snore.

"With…normal…my…pizza." He does, however, talk in his sleep.

Then he rolls over, and I suddenly don't mind the talking. For someone who works in an office…lab…whatever you would call the CZC, he sure does have a good body. And why do I feel so scummy just sitting here staring at him?

All right, I need to get out of here, anyway. I have work in the morning. He probably does, too, actually, but he's at home. It'll be easy for him to get up and get going. I'm not big on showing up in last night's outfit.

I do my best to slip out of bed gently, and considering that Terry doesn't wake up, I seemingly did a pretty good job. Now I get the fun task of finding all of my clothes in the dark.

Thankfully, I have a fairly good idea where I stripped them off as we stumbled our way to the bed. Huh, come to think of it I might have come across a little over anxious. Not that he seemed to complain.

"…no I'm gonna…pizza…tomorrow morning."

Well, he certainly has a one track mind—or dream I suppose—and it doesn't seem to be about me. My eyebrow goes up wondering if that is a good thing or not. Looking down, I'm not that bad, am I?

Grabbing a handful of my clothes I work my way to the bathroom. The door clicks behind me as I turn on the lights. Immediately I'm tempted to turn them back off. A quick turn sideways reminds me that I should be doing a few more sit-ups and maybe taking a few more stairs.

I think I hear myself sigh as I move back to putting on my clothes.

Popping back out of the bathroom I look over at Terry still fast asleep on the bed. It would be easy to just go out the door and head home. Just be another face in his past. Wouldn't be the first time I'd done such a thing, actually—but then he rolls over and I see his face, and I find myself smiling.

Before I know it, I'm beside the bed, slowly moving to sit down next to him.

"Hey," I whisper. My hand reaches out and I gently run my fingers over his upper arm. "Terry?"

He rolls back towards me and I see his eyes fluttering open. He smiles that damn pretty smile. "Hey." He looks at me and sees my state of dress and the smile goes away. "You leaving?"

"Yeah. I need to go home. I've got work in the morning." I smile back down at him. "I just wanted to say good-bye and thank you for a wonderful time."

He adjusts himself, sitting up in the bed and gathering the covers up around him. "Well, it doesn't have to be good-bye. I'd really like to see you again." He rubs the back of his neck with his right hand, which makes him seem slightly vulnerable—in a good way. "I mean, if you want."

Crap. "Yeah. Yeah, I'd like that." What the hell did I just say? Oh well, go with it. I laugh. "Maybe we can go have some pizza sometime."

"Pizza?" His head pulls back. "Uh, yeah, I guess. I'm not a big fan actually. Which makes me a freak, I know."

I probably blink a couple of times. "Wow. Then I guess you were having a nightmare. You kept talking about pizza in your sleep."

It's very dark in the room, so I can't be sure, but I would swear that his face blanches slightly. "I was? Uh, yeah, I…I guess I was having a nightmare."

"No worries. We can eat wherever you like. I was just thinking it might be nice to have dinner. Talk a bit." I feel my hand playing at the collar of my shirt.

"Sounds like a good idea to me. How's Saturday sound to you?" he asks.

"I have no plans." Sadly, that's true.

His face brightens up. "Well, now you do. Hold on." He opens the drawer on his bedside table and pulls out a pad and pen. He actually keeps something like that in his bedside table? All mine has in the top drawer is a bunch of magazines I've read and meant to throw away, along with some candy wrappers and…well, I have no idea, really. I won't mention what's in the bottom drawer.

He hands me the slip of paper and I immediately see his phone number scribbled down on it.

"Give me a call tomorrow or Saturday. We can get together that night and do dinner or whatever. I'm sure by then I'll have a good suggestion for a place to eat." He rubs his eye, covering the right side of his face with his hand.

"Okay. Right now why don't you go back to sleep and I'll head home. Like I said, I have work tomorrow." I remind myself as much as him.

"Yeah, same for me." His hand falls away from his face and finds its way to the back of my palm. Instinctively I turn mine over and let the two of them embrace. "So, call me Saturday?"

"I will." I don't wait for him. I bend over and bring my lips to his. It's soft and delicate and oh-so-tempting to make me want to crawl right back into bed. Luckily, I have enough strength to pull back—eventually. "I'll call you on Saturday."

"Great. I look forward to it." Damn that smile. I swear it even smells good.

I stand up and walk towards the bedroom door. "I'll lock the door as I leave. Good night."

"Good night." For a moment I think he's about to get out of bed and follow me, but he doesn't and I'm glad. It's already tough enough to leave without having him standing next to me.

The trek to the front door is quick and clear, and for a moment I marvel at the fact that he keeps a clean house on top of everything else, but I make it outside and into the night.

You would think that the whole zombie situation would change the way that people would act late at night, make them more fearful for their safety or something, but it hasn't been a factor at all. Really, our safety is at a constant higher rate of concern, so day or night doesn't play heavily into it.

The one thing that does keep people at bay during the night is the sound. Even at a great distance the noises the zombies create carry though the damp, dark air, and it's rather unsettling to most. For me, the odd low sound they seem to create—not exactly a moan, but not too far off—isn't that bad. I deal with it every day on a very close basis, so hearing it at a distance just tells me they aren't nearby. I can live with that.

During the drive home I can feel the stupid grin on my face that won't go away. I'm just not sure whether or not that's a good thing.

Chapter Five

"What do you mean they aren't eating?"

I'm hoping that my question comes off more upset than panicking. Especially since this is the first thing that I've heard since showing up at work.

"Just what I said: they aren't eating the cabbage," Dave says in a far too calm manner. "Not every one, mind you, but well over half, I'd wager."

"But we've still got cabbage!" I look over my shoulder to check. "We do still have cabbage, right?"

"Tons. Literally," Dave reassures me. He was nice enough to meet me at the entrance, which I should have taken as a bad sign, I suppose.

"Then why aren't they eating it? They were eating it yesterday. This isn't the way that they do things. The zombies have never not eaten something until we've run out of it!" There we go. That's my full-on panic voice—along with a double negative. "What are we doing about it?"

Dave sighs. I assume that's because he's trying to remain calm and not trying to ignore me. "I told Juan, and he's passed it up along the appropriate path. I guess he's waiting to hear back from somebody about it."

"You guess?" That might have been a little louder than I intended. "Aren't you following up on it? How can you be this calm?"

"Well, because of what I'm going to show you." There's something in the sound of his voice that's actually more unsettling than the news that the zombies have stopped eating.

"Please tell me you want to show me something that is just so happy that I won't be able to help but smile and feel good about the world." Yeah, that's not going to happen.

I can see what's happening before he says a word about it. The advantage of working in a mostly open space, I suppose. Just outside of The Mouth lies a massive horde of zombies—doing nothing. They aren't moving up to the feeding outlets or really doing much of anything. They're just standing there, shuffling slightly.

"There you go," Dave says as though he's revealed a great secret suddenly. "That's why."

"How long have they been like this?" Dave stops, but I keep walking, which, of course, causes him to step alongside me as well.

"All night. Well, basically. Ever since they stopped feeding, anyway, which was round about eleven or so. At least that we noticed, anyway." I see Dave rubbing his chin with his hand. I'm still not sure why some people seem to believe that will help them remember something, but, hey, if it works for you, who am I to complain?

"Okay, great. They aren't becoming violent, which is really good news, but," I glance over at Dave, "shouldn't you still have followed up with Juan by now?"

He gives me that look like he's just discovered a new smell and isn't sure what to think of it. "Well, maybe I was waiting for you to get here. I needed to keep an eye on our guests in case things did go bad. If he had any news he probably would have come told me, anyway. Now that you are here, though," his head jags back towards the main office, "I'll go find out what's happening. You stay here and keep an eye out, just to be safe."

"Right." My gaze wander across the field of barely moving figures. "I think I can cover this part." Chances are I was being a bit of a jerk there, and I really do like Dave, so I give him a quick smile. He gets the message and starts his trek towards the center of the facility and Juan's office.

A few seconds later, I find myself alone, staring out at the herd of zombies. Shadows turn in the growing dawn, tricking the eye with both shape and color. I like to watch the changing light, if for no other reason than it keeps me distracted from the fact that it's still too damn early in the morning. One by one, the figures change, altered by the sun as it creeps higher into the sky.

It's the light that makes a huge difference with the zombies. Most of the time that I'm watching them the sun sits high, and there is no mystery to their appearance. You see the flaws and all of the, admittedly, rather gruesome details they have to offer. At night it's the exact opposite. You can't see what is and, more importantly, isn't there on their bodies, so you fill in the details accordingly, whether accurate or not. That's how nightmares are made.

And then there's the in-between times. Dusk and dawn present a totally different show, and I'm lucky enough to be there for both, most of the time. At those moments, even figures as misshapen as these walking dead take on an ethereal quality, becoming nigh-angelic in their own way. Especially this morning, where they aren't even walking in their normal slow meander, but just waving back and forth like wheat on the wind. For all too brief a moment they become noble ghosts of lives gone by, now returned.

The light doesn't stop however, and the ghosts fade away to become very corporeal figures of death once more. One by one, they turn from something wondrous to another thing far more disturbing. I watch the sun touch them in turn, until my eyes lock upon a single figure.

It's my brown-haired friend. The tall gent with a thing for showing off his food. Only now, he's not showing anything to anyone. Like all the other zombies he's empty handed, but he is doing one thing they are not: he's looking around.

At first I laugh. I mean, what the heck could he be looking for? It's not like there are that many options for him in the world these days. Less for him than folks like me, even. Still, there is a look in the space where his eyes should be that says something to me. It gives me that one split second to consider my options and what is going on, and whether or not I should do something.

Which is to say, it is at that moment I became a complete idiot.

It wasn't exactly difficult to find a head of cabbage. Hundreds of opportunities lay little more than an arms reach away, and with only a couple of steps and a broad sweep of my arm I had a couple of heads in hand and was walking towards the edge of the facility.

Now, with the exception of when gates are opened, the entire place is sort of, I don't know, walled up inside a heavy gauge wire fence. At least as thick as anything you would see at a prison facility, and maybe a lot more. As I mentioned, though, there are gates. Some are large enough to allow for trucks to back up and be unloaded to the freight floor, while others are simply the size for a single person to pass through, and those smaller ones are scattered throughout the facility.

And one of them leads right out into the mass of zombies.

Granted, it is still about five feet off the ground, but there are stairs down. After I open the gate, I don't feel the need to rush down the stairs, though. I have a nice, clear line to my target already. So, I rear back, and doing my best impression of a major leaguer, toss my best fastball at Curly—as I affectionately now think of the zombie in question.

The cabbage falls about five feet short of him and bounces off to one side, not even drawing Curly's notice. Another reminder that my father wanted me to be a boy and I never did have the desire to play sports, much to his dismay. What I did have— rather, do still have—is far more courage and less sense than I need.

So, when I walk down the stairs and out into the gathered zombie ensemble I don't give it too much thought. The people screaming after me obviously do, though. To be honest, they are over reacting—even if I was being stupid. Over ninety percent of the time the zombies are harmless directly, causing more problems from the potential diseases they carry than anything. Of course that ten percent of the time tends to be when they don't have something to eat, so…well, let's not think about that.

A few steps in and I'm reminded of the main reason why moving among the undead is something I usually consider a bad idea. The stench of rotting flesh and pure decay almost knocks me square on my ass, and I reflexively throw my hand up over my mouth and hurry my pace.

From a closer view, Curly is a little less attractive than he was from a distance. There is a large gap on the right side of his neck that keeps his head constantly teetering over towards that side, and only one of his eyes is still in his head. It looks as though Curly didn't quite make it to the dry decay stage, and still has a bit of mold gathered on his skin.

Nonetheless, I'm well within range now, and with an underhand motion, I casually toss my second cabbage his way—and, naturally, it bounces off his chest and rolls back towards me. I watch Curly's eyes—or eye, rather—as it travels from the cabbage that struck him back to the person who threw the assaulting vegetable his way. And suddenly I have his full, undivided attention. Lucky me.

Glancing towards the ground for a moment, I locate the cabbage and drop down to grab it. By the time I'm back upright, Curly has walked up on me, now standing barely more than an arm's length away. Naturally, I do what anyone would do in that situation: I hand him the cabbage. Thankfully, he takes it—and then drops it again right away. The vegetable gift does seem to stop him, though, so at least it had one good result.

"Cici!" Dave's bellow cuts through the haze and hits me from behind. My head spins around and I see him halfway down the stairs, motioning for me to come back. The sensible part of me thinks this is a wonderful idea, but that same annoying part that caused me to run out into the middle of this horde has my feet cemented in place.

"Dave! What food do we have?" That's a good question, I think.

"What? Just run back here!"

I look over at Curly, who's gone back to looking around and staying relatively still. I feel that breath I was holding leave my body as I turn back to Dave. "Just answer the damn question! What have we got besides cabbage? Anything?"

"Uh…cereal. Why? Get over here, dammit!" He seems agitated, not that I blame him.

"Get me some!" I take a few steps his way, but not for the purpose of leaving.

"I'm coming to get you!" He takes another step down the stairs, but I don't let it go any further.

"No! Look, I'm fine." To illustrate my point I spin in a circle slowly—which also gives me a chance to make sure that none of the zombies are actually moving up on me. "Get me the cereal and then I'll come back up, okay?"

Watching the person behind him run off, I'm guessing my cereal is on the way. I wonder what type of cereal it is? Puffed rice? Corn flakes? Shredded wheat? I'll find out soon enough, I suppose.

The guy who ran off shows back up with another two people in tow, each of them sporting a big box of cereal. Dave grabs on and holds it out at arm's length.

"Now come on back, Cici," he says in a calm, even tone. "I got your cereal right here."

Wow. He's not very good at the whole tricking-me-back-so-he-can-grab-me kind of thing. Still, I've got to give him credit for trying.

"Just toss it here, Dave, okay? It'll just take a minute."

There must have been something in the tone of my voice, because it only takes him a handful of seconds before he arcs the box towards me in a long, underhand throw. I have to take a couple of steps in towards him, but I manage to catch it before it hits the ground.

I don't waste any time. As I rush back towards Curly I bring the box up and get a good look at it. Corn flakes. Should have known.

There are lots and lots of zombies out here. Most of them are staying still and definitely far enough away that they don't pose an immediate threat, but the fact that I'm completely surrounded basically takes away any security I might have felt from proximity.

Getting a job with F.O.O.D.Z. is like starting most anywhere else: you get to have a wonderful and entertaining orientation seminar. We are instructed in the best ways to move and interact with zombies, but those lessons are rarely put to use, as the easiest—and most highly advised—strategy for dealing with them is to simply stay away. Keep them in the distance. Don't challenge them in any way. Or, to put it another way, exactly the opposite of what I'm doing by stepping to within sudden striking distance of one.

Curly looks at me with his one eye, and I swear he looks confused. Or possibly annoyed, so I'm actually hoping for confused. The box that I hold out for him draws his attention, but only long enough for him to further progress from confused to annoyed.

"Take it," I urge softly. "It's food. It's…um…it's…." What the hell do I tell him about this? "It's…new. It's fresh and exciting. It's got, uh, crunch." A quick shake of the box provides some accompaniment for my ravings, but the face staring at me—the hideous, decaying face—is still looking lost. If that's possible, anyway.

Turning my eye to the box, I think I understand why. Cabbage looks like food. It smells like food. This, on the other hand, looks and smells like a cardboard box.

The cardboard shreds easily in my hand, revealing the plastic bag of breakfast fare inside. I make short work of it, too, tearing it wide and grabbing a handful of the corn product. Holding it out towards Curly to make sure that he can see it, I then pull my hand back and take a huge bite of cereal. These are not sugar frosted. Most likely one of the more childish holdovers I have is only really liking super sweet breakfast cereals, but I'm not going to let him know that.

My smile is as wide as it can go, filling my whole face with a forced expression of happiness. If Curly is able to tell the difference between a lie and the truth, I might be in trouble here. Once more I hold out the box of cereal, but this time the contents and the means to enjoy them have been revealed.

It might have been a minute, or it might have been a few seconds, but eventually Curly's hands surround the sides of the box and take it from my grasp. My heartbeat is audible, probably to more than just me at the moment, and I have to remind myself to keep breathing.

Then, with all the grace you would expect from a corpse, Curly reaches his hand down into the box and returns with a handful of cereal. He stares at it and his head lolls off to the right a little more than usual. My hand motions up a couple of times, trying with all of my non-existent magical power to get him to go ahead and take a bite.

And then he does. His hand just moves up to his mouth and he takes a huge bite of the flakes, about a third of them dropping to the ground as they slip away from his grip, but most of them go into the mouth. I watch him chew for a minute and then I take a cautious step backwards, watching and waiting for that hopeful moment.

Slowly, the hand goes back in and he takes another bite, and as he does I turn to look around. They are still standing, unmoving and oblivious. I look back at Curly. He's got maybe his third or fourth handful of flakes going into his mouth, and I see him looking at me. His hand goes up and displays the box of cereal towards me.

"Corn flakes," I say gently. "They're corn flakes."

His mouth continues to macerate the pulp in his mouth, but that doesn't keep him from responding, "Flaaaaakes."

And that's when I see a zombie turn towards him—and then others. No point in being here now, and I turn and sprint towards the dock and the very, very nervous looking Dave. His windmill arm is doing its best to speed me up, but right now I'm not sure I could possibly have more adrenaline running through my body.

"Get more!" I shout as I continue to sprint. "Get them loaded in The Mouth. Get ready to distribute the corn flakes!"

"What?" His head pops back like I slapped him.

"Just do it, okay! Get the damn cereal to The Mouth!" I reach the dock and his arm grabs me and yanks me up onto the stairs in a single motion.

"What the hell were you thinking!" he screams in my face. I'm not big on being yelled at, actually. "Those monsters could have torn you apart! Have you lost your damned mind?"

"Dave!" I yell back at him, but it doesn't slow him down.

"Zombies are unpredictable. They could have just as easily torn you limb from limb as stand there staring at you like that!"

"Dave!" I grab his head and turn it back out towards Curly. Several zombies have gathered around him, and he's holding the box up for all of them to see. "Get. More. Cereal."

I can feel him blink. His head is facing away from me, but I swear I can feel him blink. As I lower my hands his head comes back around to look at me, and I don't think I've ever seen anyone—or any dog or cat or other—look at me with more confusion. "What…?"

"Just do it, okay?" My voice turns to the soft version. Honey over vinegar and all that.

"Yeah. Yeah, okay." He looks up at the other workers gathered at the top of the stairs. I see Juan there, too. "Get the cereal to The Mouth. Just to be safe." He looks at Juan. "That's okay, right?"

"Uh, well, we'll make it work. Assuming it works," he answers.

I'm not sure if I was the first one to hear it, but I'm pretty sure I was the first one to look out at the gathered undead as they began to drone their new favorite word. "Flaaaaaakes."

They began to shuffle towards The Mouth, looking for their next meal. I can't help myself. I smile, proud of being able to avert this crisis and get the zombies under control, if even for a moment.

I wish I had known then just how much I had totally screwed up my life with that one, single action.

Chapter Six

"I don't believe you."

Julie has a tone sitting somewhere between jealousy and trying to make sure that I'm not just trying to pull one over on her.

"It's true," I tell her calmly. "I was able to avert a crisis. I'm a hero."

The smile I've got on my face is probably a little too obnoxious—but I kind of want it that way. It's not every day that a girl like me gets to brag about doing something that potentially could have saved the day.

"How? How did you do it?" She leans forward, trying to get a little closer to me and make sure the crowd noise at Tatters doesn't drown out what I'm about to tell her.

I just wish I had a better answer for her.

"Um, dumb luck, honestly. I saw this zombie and he was acting weird and I just…took a chance." My shoulders go up in a half-shrug to accompany the brilliance of my tale.

Her face screws up in that way that warns me to expect a lecture to follow. "I don't believe you. I'm sorry. It's one thing to tell me you got lucky, but…not like this. You don't just get lucky by running out into a horde of zombies and convincing one of them to eat breakfast cereal."

That's the problem with having a best friend who knows everything about you—they know everything about you.

"Okay, fine," I sigh, "there was something else." My seat in the booth suddenly feels very uncomfortable. "Back when the world was…the world, like you know, I did promotions for the travel agency. No big deal, but I had to learn my boss. Y'know?"

"Everyone has to do that, honey. Get to your point."

"No, I mean I had to learn who my boss was. It was always changing. Because I was having to make different people happy for different things, I had to learn the cues to figure out exactly who I was trying to impress. Who was my boss."

Julie nods slowly, so I'm hoping that she gets it, but just to be safe….

"Okay, it's like this. If I was told to push, say, a cruise package, I have to find the cruise lines and get a deal too good to be passed up. That meant that my new boss, so to speak, was the woman running the cruise line we almost always used because I knew what she wanted. I was able to read her and follow her lead to get the best out of her and the best for our clients." My face scrunches up in hope—or frustration, I'm not sure. "Does that make sense?"

"It…does. Basically, you're saying that you had to figure out who you were selling to," Julie answers.

"No. Not exactly, anyway. The whole point wasn't that I was selling to them, but getting them to sell to me. And the only one who could do that was the person in charge. The boss.

Anyone below them and they couldn't make a decision. They were the go between that bounced back and forth with me and the boss, so I had to get past them, read who was in charge, and talk to the boss." I shrug again, this time more purposefully. "Curly was the boss."

"Curly? Who's Curly?" Oh yeah, I might need to explain that one.

"He's the boss. The zombie that I gave the corn flakes."

She has that look. The one that tells me that I'm crazy, but there's no way that she's going to say that to my face, either because she loves me or because she's afraid I really am crazy and will do something insane. I'm sticking with the love theory, personally.

"Boss zombie. Named Curly." She says it slow and deliberate, to make sure I hear my own words.

"I know. It sounds crazy, and it probably is, but it worked. So, I'm going to go back to my original theory." I smile at her like I can only smile at my best friend. "I got lucky."

"You got lucky?" That voice doesn't belong to Julie. I turn to see a pretty face staring back at me. "Should I leave you alone?"

"Terry, hey. What are you doing here?" I think the tone of my voice just went up an octave.

"Well," he raises his glass, "I thought I would come get a drink. May I join you?"

Hell yes you can join me! If you don't I'll get pissed, actually. "Sure."

Scooting over, I make room for him beside me. I'm not moving to the other side of the table this time. I feel his weight next to me as he settles into place, and I try not to act too happy about it. Looking across the table at Julie's face, though, I don't think I pulled off the subtlety.

"So, what was this about you getting lucky?" Terry asks, glancing over at me.

"She saved us all from a hungry horde of zombies." Julie nods as though this is a simple fact.

"Oh, did you?" There is a little swagger to Terry's voice as he pulls back to look at me. Oh, it is on.

"What? You don't believe it?" My eyes move up and down his body as I talk.

"I never said that!" He takes a quick swig of his drink and sets it back down. "In this day and age you can never take that sort of thing lightly."

"Well, let me tell you, mister, I am more than capable of handling a few zombies on my own." It seems appropriate to reciprocate, so I throw back a little of my drink. "How many have you dealt with all at once?"

His eyes shift, moving away from me for a second while his mouth hangs open. He doesn't say the first words that come to him and settles for his second thought. "I'm not a zombie type. I stay as far away from them as I can."

"At the CZC?" Julie asks. "How can you avoid them working down there?"

He laughs and runs his finger around the rim of his glass. "We work with theoretical, not actual. So, in a virtual, clinical sense I've dealt with thousands, I suppose. In the real world, not so much."

"You've never faced down a zombie?" Everyone has done that at least once, right?

"Not the way that you're implying. I've seen them and I've stayed clear of them. That's face down enough for me." A single nod emphasizes his statement. "But what about this horde? What did you do?"

"Well—" I'm considering exactly what I want to tell him, but never get my own opportunity.

"She fed them!" Julie can be so helpful sometimes. "Just like that."

Terry's eyes move from Julie and back to me a few times. "Uh, yeah, well, you work at a F.O.O.D.Z. station, right? That's kinda what you do."

"It is, yes," I answer slowly, giving Julie a glance, "but this was a little different."

"How so?" He actually shifts in his seat so that he's turned towards me a little more. As he does, his hand comes up to rest behind my neck on the seat back. I feel the hairs back there rise to try to meet him.

"Uh, well, I just…." Concentrate, Cici! "They stopped eating cabbage—that's what they've been eating lately, cabbage— anyway, they stopped eating it and we had to do something. I saw this one zombie, Curly, and I gave him some corn flakes and that did the trick."

His eyes narrow, and his pretty face turns slightly rugged. That's not helping. "What do you mean that did the trick? What happened?"

"They ate the cereal!" Julie jumps back in, and I'm kind of grateful this time.

He looks over at her and then back to me. "Wait, you're telling me that you were able to dictate what they ate?"

"Yeah, I guess." That does pretty much sum it up, actually.

"Okay, okay, um," he shifts completely, now sitting square towards me—and moving his hand back to his side, "let's go over this step-by-step. What happened?"

I step through the motions in my head, putting them in order as best I can. "I saw a zombie acting oddly, and I named him Curly. The next day they weren't eating cabbage, so I took some corn flakes out to Curly. He ate them and then the other zombies joined in. Though one of them looked a little annoyed when he tried to eat the toy that came in one box."

"That's…that's not…." His eyes glaze over. Something inside is having trouble with what I'm saying. "It doesn't work that way."

With a deep breath, I give him my casual shrug. "Did this time. I'm just thankful we had something else to offer them."

The whirring of gears is almost audible from his brain. "You ran out of cabbage—"

"No," I correct him instantly. "We still had plenty of cabbage, they just stopped eating it."

"You had an instance of nutrient retraction, initiated by the subject, and then were able to redirect their focus to a new food source. That's…that's…." He went into science mode, I think.

"Weird." It's the easiest way to sum it up, actually.

"No." Or I could be wrong. "No, this is…. Can I come see this zombie? Watch what he does?"

"Uh, sure, I guess. I'll have to clear it with my boss, but given the circumstances, I can't imagine him saying no. I can't promise he's going to be there. Curly, I mean, not my boss. My boss should be there."

And then that smile comes back, but this one has a slightly different edge to it. "That would be wonderful. I'd love to see this in action."

"It's just watching a bunch of zombies eat, but if that makes you happy…." No, seriously, if that makes you happy, I'm good with it. "I guess it'll be your first chance to see some zombies up close." I lean over slightly. "They do get pretty close, just so you're warned."

"I think I'll be fine with that." He takes another sip of his drink, and I match him.

"So, why do zombies have to eat, anyway?" Julie asks, reminding me that she's at the table with us. "I mean, what's going to happen if they don't? Are they going to die?"

Terry turns back, sitting more normally in the booth, but with all the adjusting he's had to move a little and he's pressed up against my thigh—not that I'm complaining. "That's a very good question, actually." He shakes his head. "I have no idea. I've wondered the same thing, but can't find any conclusive research on the subject. There have been studies, of course, but no answers as to why they still eat food. At least not yet."

"Well, maybe they just like eating." Julie puts the straw in her mouth and has a sip of her club soda. The rebel.

"That's one explanation, I suppose." He laughs and takes another sip of his drink. I'm smelling fruit, which makes me think that it's one of those party drinks that should have a little paper umbrella sticking out of it.

Glancing down at my whiskey tonic with a wedge of lime in it and realize that is about as fruity as my cocktails get. I can't help but smile a little. Even as my hand moves out and comes to rest on his thigh.

His hand moves over mine and we lace fingers.

51

Chapter Seven

"Terry, this is Juan. Juan, Terry."

They shake hands in that guy way. Y'know, with their arms and hands a little too flexed for some reason.

"Thanks for letting me come by," Terry says in that easy tone of his.

"Well, I don't know what we'll be able to do to help, but anything that we can do, we will." I told Juan about Terry and why he wanted to come by, and got it all cleared, and in the process created a little more excitement. It made us feel kind of important for a change.

"I've already told Terry everything that I could," I offer up, "but he still wanted to come by and see things for himself. Not that there is anything to see."

"Still no sign of him?" Terry asks.

"Nope." Sadly, Curly hasn't been seen around here since two days after we started on the corn flake feedings. I've been trying to keep an eye out, but nothing. I even suggested that Terry wait until I see him again and I'd call him in, but he said that wouldn't work. So, here he is.

"Well, hopefully we'll see him today." At least he's optimistic.

"Let me give you the nickel tour." I'm tempted to grab Terry's arm and lead him, but I'm trying to keep this professional, so I just sweep my arm out and offer a suggested direction of travel.

"I'll get back to work. Let me know if you need anything. It was nice meeting you, Terry," Juan extends his hand again, and they go through the ritual handshake one more time, this time with a short nod at the end of it.

"Seems like a nice guy," Terry says just as Juan gets out of earshot.

"He is." I walk, letting Terry fall in beside me. "He was here when I got hired. Helped me learn the ropes and how to deal with everything. Dave—he's the guy who works my job the shift opposite me—he's helped a lot, too. Got me past the feeling of dread every time I saw one of them." I motion off the dock to the zombies mulling about.

"They look so peaceful," Terry says.

"You sound jealous." It's true. His tone came off that way to me.

"Oh no! I appreciate being alive, don't get me wrong." He chuckles, whether it's to comfort him or me I'm not sure. "They just don't look like monsters right now."

"I never see them that way. To me they aren't monsters, they're just...zombies. It's weird, I know. I suppose it's because I do deal with them so often. I understand what they are and how they are going to act most of the time—well, as much as you can, I suppose. It's like someone who works with sharks or something. They understand how dangerous they are, but they also realize that those things aren't monsters, they're just what they are."

"I suppose so." He chuckles again, and I have the same questions about it.

"Still, I understand." I walk over to the edge of the dock and stop, looking out towards The Mouth and the zombies slowly funneling in. The sun is up and high, and the temperature is rather nice today. Thankfully we're past the ridiculous heat of the summer here, and heading into fall. It's my favorite time of the year in these parts. Some may like spring, but the pollen around Atlanta is stupid. Things actually turn green because of it. I'm not talking about the plants growing, but things like furniture, your house, or your body if you linger too long becoming covered in pollen and turn green. Seriously. "When they are acting like this, things almost seem normal. It's like the world hasn't changed and we can just enjoy a nice day."

"You don't? Enjoy a nice day, I mean?" We both keep our eyes out on the zombies as they pass through the line.

"Depends. Weather can help a day, but if you're having a crappy one, you're having a crappy one. And some of the best days of my life have come on grey, rainy afternoons." I finally look over to him. "I'm not a slave to weather."

"Neither am I. I just like to enjoy a sunny day when I can. Don't know when the next one will come along." He looks back at me and smiles.

"It'll come. They always do." I smile back.

We've been spending a lot of time together since we met almost three weeks ago, now. Last weekend I actually stayed over at his place for the first time. It felt good, and to be honest, that kind of worries me. I don't want to have these feelings. Not now.

He looks back out to The Mouth and takes a deep breath. "So, what are their names?"

That causes a few blinks from me. "I beg your pardon?"

"The zombies. Which ones have names?" He points vaguely out to the crowd and my eyes follow.

"Uh, none."

"Really?" He turns back to me, and I meet his eyes. "You just named the one?"

"Well, yeah. I never saw the point."

"So, he's the only one you saw with any unique traits? There aren't even some that have a unique look to them that might cause a nickname? I'm sure the folks studying sharks come up with names for them." He's got a point.

"Yeah, I just…." My shoulders shrug and I feel a little small. "I never thought about it. I try not to think about it, I guess."

"Why not?" Oh no. Don't go into this.

I take a deep breath and ready myself. "You're talking to a woman who's hair is hitting halfway down her neck. I can't decide if I want it to grow out or cut it short, so it's just hanging there in between."

"So?" He keeps looking at me.

"I don't like to make choices like that. Decide something."

"How is coming up with a nickname deciding something?" His whole body turns towards me, but I keep facing off the dock.

I feel myself swallow. "I'm from Nashville. I haven't mentioned that, have I?" I glance at him and then look back out to The Mouth. "I moved down here right after everything went to hell. Maybe not the best timing, but I had to do it. My brother is still pissed at me."

"Why?" His voice is soft and gentle, but prodding in the right way.

"My parents live up there. Or did, anyway." Please understand. Please.

"Okay, so?" Dammit.

"So, they…they don't live there anymore. They passed a few years back." This isn't the right time for this conversation. I should be sitting down and he should be holding me. Comforting me. Not standing apart on a concrete slab.

"Oh. Did you…?"

"No." I shake my head. "I left before I could. Before the odd chance might have happened. I honestly don't even know if they ever came back. I don't want to know, either. Nashville turned from the place that I grew up to the place that might have my dead parents walking around it, so I left. Took a bus to Atlanta and been here since."

"Risky. Things are scary now. They were terrifying back when it first happened." He's keeping his voice low enough to not be heard by anyone but me.

"Better than hanging around and meeting your mom in a dark alley." My voice cracks slightly, I think. I don't listen close enough to confirm it.

There is a long silence. I don't want a silence. He needs to be saying something. Why isn't he saying anything?

"You're wrong." Well, that wasn't what I was expecting. It does get me to look at him, though. I'm not sure if I'm glaring in anger or confusion.

"What?"

"About yourself. You're wrong. You make decisions. The important ones. Whether it's moving down here or running out into a group of zombies to convince them that corn flakes are the next great meal, you know when to do the right thing." His smile makes me believe him—almost.

"Tell that to my brother. He says that I abandoned him."

"Did you? Was there something that you needed to be there for? Did you leave him alone minding the farm or something like that?"

A shake of my head is the best answer, but I elaborate anyway. "No. He is—or at least was, I'm not sure now—the manager of a grocery store. Worked his ass off, but never did anything else. No family except me, though, so I did kind of leave him alone."

"He could have followed, you know," he says. "You explained why you left?"

"Of course. I just…I don't want to be seen as a coward for it." The sigh I had been holding in finally comes out.

"That's on him, not you. You weren't running away from responsibility or something like that. It was a bad situation that might have gotten worse. There's nothing wrong with what you did." Has he practiced this? Does he always know the right thing to say?

"Have you…? Your parents, I mean?" I squeeze my eyes half-shut.

"No. I'm from Portland. They brought me in for my professional skills. I've got no family anywhere near here. My mom and dad are still alive, too. Sisters as well. Two of them." He nods to the side, as though pointing to his familial home somehow.

"Are you close?"

"Yeah. Always been a tight family, actually, but that doesn't mean anything. Not about you." His eyes narrow as well, but in a different way. "You live your own life. Don't let others become the reason you are doing anything. You'll know in your heart what is right for you."

"I hope you're right." I sniff. That's as close to crying as I'm going to let myself get, though.

"I am." He holds his hand out. I probably shouldn't do it, but I reach over and grab it for a moment, giving it a bit of a firm squeeze before letting go.

And then I let myself have just a moment. Allow the minute or so to pass where I'm just standing there with him, ignoring the world and feeling that everything is okay.

It's a good feeling.

"Tina." I finally say.

His eyes go wide. "I'm sorry? Who's Tina?"

"One of the zombies. In my head I've always called her Tina because of the way she walks around and moans like that girl from the burger restaurant animated tv show." I take a breath and feel my lungs grow. "So, yeah, I have given them nicknames, sometimes. I just don't tell anyone."

"I think it's safe to tell people." He chuckles, but this time I know why.

"I don't want to come across as unprofessional." It's a serious job, after all.

"You feed zombies for a living. I think having nicknames could only help the situation."

He's got a point.

"Come on." I turn back towards the center of the dock. "I've still got a lot of places left to show you. And we need to try to find Curly if we can."

"Or Tina. I'd like to meet any zombie that you know personally."

Okay, now it's my turn to chuckle.

Chapter Eight

It's funny how the night can cause us to react differently to the same event during daylight.

If we see someone walking down the street during the day we don't give it a second look. That same person walking down the same street in the middle of the night raises an eyebrow. Same thing if a car drives by, too. A phone call during the day is met with nothing but a glance at the phone long enough to pick it up and answer. If you get a call in the middle of the night, though, you'll likely jump up and scramble for the phone in either a slight daze or a panic, depending on your personality. Of course, that's if you keep your phone near your bed while you're sleeping, because if you don't, then it doesn't bother you at all.

You don't get that option with a loud banging on the door, though. That sort of sound carries through the whole house and tends to create a rush of emotional response.

Which is why I feel rather cranky as I head to the door. I glanced at the clock as I half-tumbled out of bed and it was telling me that it was after 4:00 am, which means that no matter what happens here, I'm going to be angry, because it will seem like I just got back to sleep when my alarm goes off, no matter how much time really has passed. Hell, I don't think I actually fell asleep until after 2:00, anyway.

At least I still have the sense to look through the peep hole to see who—or maybe even what—is knocking at the door. Thankfully, it's a who—or a pair of who, actually, one man and one woman—but any more precise a description of who is a total mystery.

Putting the chain on the door I crack it open, peeking my head around from the back carefully.

"Hello?" The slight crack in my voice is a total accident, but hopefully it reminds them of the hour.

"Hello!" The man talks first. "We are so very, very sorry to be bothering you this hour, but we are trying to keep to a tight schedule, which means that we had to come by very early. I hope you understand."

My nose wrinkles up into my brow as I give him a slight sneer. Both he and his female companion are dressed in black slacks, black button shirts, and black jackets. Rather formal looking, if untraditionally so.

"I...what?" That pretty much covers all my questions.

"Ms. Cole?" The woman asks, and I turn right to her. "You are Cassandra Cole, correct?"

Like the man, her tone and demeanor are annoying. It's far too early in the morning to be that damn cheery.

"Yeah." I nod and feel the sudden need to pull my robe a little tighter around me.

"Oh good, we would have been totally embarrassed if we had the wrong apartment." She actually does a fake wipe of sweat from her forehead as she says that.

"We've made that mistake before," the man says with a light laugh.

"What?" I stand up a little straighter and try to look past the two, scanning for anyone else and finding no one. "What is this about? Who are you?"

"Well, I'm Alice," the woman points to herself and then over to her companion, "and this is Alex. We're here to talk to you about certain events."

That didn't sound a little odd. Not at all. "What events? What's going on?"

"Ms. Cole, if you would let us inside," the man, Alex, apparently, takes over speaking, "we're not comfortable talking about it like this." His arm gestures widely around him. "Out in the open, I mean."

Yeah, that's not going to be enough. "I'm sorry, no. It's four in the morning, and I don't know you at all. I need you to leave, or else I'll have to call the police."

"Oh, no. No, don't do that, Ms. Cole. We really don't want any undue trouble." If it weren't for the outfit, I would swear she was a college cheerleader of some sort. Light brown hair pulled into a ponytail, and pretty fit from what I can see. Maybe a little tall, though. Both she and the man are around six feet tall each. She might even have an inch or so on him.

"That would be bad, Ms. Cole. We don't want to cause a scene." He's kind of got that same vibe, honestly. Red haired—dark red, not clown red—male cheerleader, with freckles and everything.

Time to end this. "No. Good night."

The door makes it most of the way closed—most, but not all. At first I think they've jammed something in the gap, but then

I see Alice's hand. The only thing keeping the door open is her. I put my shoulder into it. It doesn't budge.

"I'm really sorry it's coming to this, Ms. Cole." I watch her turn to Alex and give him a nod.

"Already working on it," is his reply. Beyond her I think I see him fiddling with a device of some kind that he's pulled out of his pocket. A phone or something.

And then I jump back. Not intentionally, mind you, but because I was launched that way. The only thing that stops Alice from walking into the apartment is the heavy-duty chain that I've got on the door.

"Wow!" She actually sounds excited. "I've got to compliment you, Ms. Cole. You've got the chain bolted into the actual wall studs and not just the frame. Very good! Much more protective."

Even though she's being amazingly complimentary considering the situation, I still turn and bolt for the bedroom and my phone. I do make a mental note to thank Julie's husband Mike for installing the extra security on my front door.

The door rattles as she slams against it again, and I swear that I feel the whole apartment shake. My hand fumbles on my phone, shaking as it comes up and I attempt to unlock it. It takes three tries—thank you nerves—but it does unlock. My fingers quickly bring up the keypad and I hit 911—but nothing happens. I do it again, with the same non-result. Each time I try the call the front door announces its pain dramatically, and I would swear that I hear the woman, Alice, cry out "Tally-ho!"

I want to laugh at that, but I'm a little too terrified at the moment. The phone is out at arms length, with me staring at it blankly. So much so, in fact, that it takes me a couple of seconds to notice that I'm not getting a cell signal. None at all, and I normally have a very strong one.

"Shit!" It is now time for me to do the traditional dance of the cell phone, where you wander around holding it in front of you waiting for signal bars to return. It's magical, truly. Normally, I would head for the front door, but right now, not so much.

The balcony is the next best option. A quick flip of the lock and I step out into the night air. Nothing. I lean out over the balcony hoping for the best and finding exactly what I don't want to see.

I live on the third floor of my building, and with the lay of the land, the drop off my balcony is almost four stories. And at that moment, about halfway up, is the man, Alex, climbing towards my balcony.

"Just relax, Ms. Cole." He sees me. "I'll be there in a minute."

I think I scream. I'm not sure, but I think I do. The front door shakes as I rush back into the room, accompanied by the distinct sound of metal screaming as it is forcefully bent. Raw instinct takes over. Fight or flight, and I'm not much of a fighter.

My bedroom door slams behind me and I fumble with the lock just long enough to hear it click. I leap to the far side of my bed, huddling down to the ground, and hating myself for being so damn scared. I live in a world where the dead have come back to life, and I can't help but be terrified of two people breaking into my house—because I have nowhere to run.

My dad would have loved this. He always preached preparedness, saying that you can never be sure. All of it stemming from when his house caught fire when he was a kid.

Fire. Wait, this is like a fire. I'm trapped in my own bedroom and just outside my door is the flame. I can't go out that way, so I have to escape. And dad, bless him, bought me my own kit.

The training he instilled in me takes over. Right below the window in my room, bolted down—without telling the landlord, of course—is the box. I open it up and get it ready. Next comes the window, which I slide up easily and smoothly. The escape ladder goes next, rattling down the side of the building—and I follow it.

One rung after another I drop down, heading to the ground. It isn't until I'm about halfway down that I realize I don't have anything. No keys, no phone, nothing. I'm completely on my own. Still, it's better than being trapped in my own apartment. I hope.

As my feet hit the ground I suddenly realize just how undressed I actually am right now. Perfect. I have nothing, not even clothes, and any second now those two are going to bust into my room and figure out what I did, so I don't really have any time.

There are basically two choices. I can run to the parking lot, screaming to my apartment complex, and try to get some help there, or I can break into the woods and go for the walking trail that leads out near the main road. I opt for the second choice. The parking lot might work, but it also is where those two will have the easiest time finding me. I'm guessing they don't know those trails like I do, and even in the dark with nothing on me I'll have an advantage.

So, I'm running. Quick as I can, semi-blindly, onto the running trail that I've been known to use more than a few times.

You know the trick about running into the woods at night? Yeah, I don't either it turns out, and I really should have known it. After all, it's what I deal with on a daily basis.

Edible Complex

I don't see them at first as much as I smell them. The putrid stench of decay that accompanies them wherever they go. There are probably two dozen of them scattered around me, moaning and moving about.

My breath catches in my throat. The fear that has been powering me yells at me to run the other way, but my brain quenches that quickly. A quick glance back confirms that thought. Both Alex and Alice have made their way down the ladder and are standing, considering their options.

And then they take their first step towards the woods.

If I run they'll hear me. They might even see me. I only have one choice. Grabbing a handful of dirt I wipe as much of it on myself and my clothes as I can and wander into the pack of zombies.

Thankfully, years of watching zombies mull about have given me a pretty good idea of how to act like one, and I do my very best impression of playing dead—while still walking.

I can't take the time to look back. With the same casual meander I walk among them, doing my best to remain calm and even, though I'm shocked that they can't hear my heartbeat. The damned muscle is trying to pound its way out of my chest, after all.

They're moving deeper into the woods, away from the trail and the parts that I know. With every step I wince slightly, feeling the rough floor of the trees biting into the soles of my feet, and fortunately I'm able to make a few moans that sound rather convincing because of it. The cries of pain, however, I have to keep to myself.

The lights of the parking lot fade into the background and I let them, hoping instead to see the light of the morning show up for me. Maybe in the daylight I can find some clues to what happened and what the hell I can do about it.

But for now, I walk with the zombies. It's the only way for me to be alive.

Chapter Nine

"What happened to you?"

I'd like to think the expression on Julie's face is worse than the one I'm wearing, but I won't be taking any bets on that.

"Long night spent walking with zombies. Can I come in?"

"Yes! Get in here!" She literally grabs me by the arm and pulls me into her house.

If I thought I looked bad when it started, I'm sure I look like a nightmare right now. The initial mud smear I gave myself got more than a little worse the longer we went on. More than once I slipped and fell, not only covering me with the lovely melange of substances that coat the forest floor, but also giving the little bit of clothing I was wearing a few rips and tears.

"Let's get you out of those things and into a hot shower!" Julie moves behind me and starts pushing me up the stairs.

"Don't you want to know why I spent the night with zombies?" Seems like the first thing I would ask.

"Of course I do, but right now getting you cleaned up and comfy is first priority. We can talk after." God, I love Julie.

Doesn't care why I'm like this, she just wants to get me fixed.

"If it wouldn't get you filthy, I would hug you so hard right now," I half say, half sob.

She doesn't answer, but I think I can feel her smile. I trudge upstairs and start to go into the guest bath, but Julie quickly redirects me.

"No, no. You get the good shower. Let's go."

I don't resist. I'm both too tired and too weak to even attempt it. Before I even know what's happening I'm standing naked under a wonderfully hot stream of water. For a few minutes I just let the water run over me, letting it wash away the outer layer of what happened. Eventually I do grab some soap and a washcloth and get to work. Shampoo follows, and I even follow the instructions this time: lather, rinse, repeat.

"How's it going, honey?" Julie's voice snaps me out of the steam-filled nirvana for a moment.

"Better. Much better." I wince slightly as I shift in the shower. "Though, can I bother you to get some medicine and some bandages for my feet. I tore them up pretty good."

"Oh God, of course!" I hear a couple of cabinet doors open and bang shut and can see her figure moving about past the steamed-up glass. And for some reason, at that moment, I feel my shoulders slip down.

I turn off the blissful shower and run my hands over my hair, squeezing out as much water as I can muster. By the time I open the door to the shower, Julie is standing there with a bath sheet in her hands.

"C'mon, let's get you dried off." I step out and she wraps it around me, letting me take over control of it and how I dry myself. She steps away and grabs a small wooden seat that was against the far wall. "Sit down on this. I want to look at those feet."

She gets no argument from me. I plop down rather ungracefully and let her take ahold of my foot.

"Oh my God! Cici, what did you do! You're feet are all cut up!" Her eyes are half sad, half panic.

"It's a long story," I mumble. "I didn't have any shoes, and I had to get away. Didn't have a choice."

"Get away? Get away from who? The zombies?" I hear a gasp. "Oh! Were you attacked by zombies?"

A half laugh comes out of me as I shake my head. "No. No, the zombies kind of saved me, actually. There was this man and woman, and they knew who I was, and they were trying to break into my apartment. I didn't have my phone so I couldn't call, and by the time I got out of the woods I really did look like a zombie and nobody would stop for me, so I walked here."

"You're not making any sense. Start at the beginning." She tends to my feet, while I do my best to mutter through the events of the night. I'm not really sure just how much detail I cover. My brain and I are not really on speaking terms at the moment. It keeps insisting that I get some sleep, but I have to remind it again and again just how tired I am. Silly brain, trying to tell me what to do. Sure you can make me float through the air and everything, but that won't stop me from bumping into clouds now, will it?

And then I'm a fox. A small, red fox, running through the woods. Behind me I hear a horn blare, followed by the braying of hounds. My eyes dart about, looking for a good passage—a hollow log or thick briar—that might throw them off of my trail, but there is nothing. All I can see is a herd of deer grazing in the distance.

I want to run with them. Perhaps even chase them myself, and by doing so avoid the hounds that are on my tail. Instead, I run into the mud, sinking down past my legs. Flailing about, I try to leap up and out of the trap, but all I do is wade forward towards the deer, each of whom is ignoring me in favor of continuing to graze.

The snapping of a twig turns my head, and I see a man and woman smiling at me, hounds waiting patiently behind them.

"Tally ho, Ms. Cole," they say in unison.

And that's when I pop up into a sitting position in bed. My heart and breath are so loud that I don't even hear the door open.

"Hey, welcome back." Julie's voice brings my breath back under my control. "How are you feeling? You were making some odd noises just now, so I was coming to check on you."

My head turns around, looking at the surroundings. I'm sitting in her bed, naked.

"What…what happened?" Everything is so lost to me.

"Well, you were telling me about what happened to you, at least a little bit, and then you very quickly went from speaking to nonsense to flat-out asleep. I was barely able to get you to my bed." She moves over and sits on the foot of the bed, her eyes never leaving me. "You had me worried. You've been out for about six hours."

"Six hours?!" My hand goes to my hair and makes it halfway through before I simply grab a handful. "Oh no. I never called into work. I was supposed to be there today. They're going to—"

"It's okay, Cici, I took care of that. Don't you go worrying now. I spoke to that Juan fellow and told him that you were really sick. He completely understood." Her smile is accompanied by a quick squeeze of my calf by her left hand.

Without waiting for me to reply she stands up and walks to the chair in the corner. "I pulled out some clothes. I don't know if they'll fit you, but I figure it's better than nothing. Go ahead and put these on and then come downstairs. I imagine that you're hungry, so I'll make you something to eat. Also, Mike came home and wants to talk to you about what happened."

"I…yeah. Yeah, that sounds good." All of it actually. The clothes. The food. And talking to Mike.

And a few minutes later I find that I was definitely right about the food. The clothes are a little ill-fitting, but they get the job done. Right now how I look isn't very high on my list of priorities. Finishing the pancakes that Julie made and getting some answers from Mike are pretty well up there, though.

"So, let me make sure I have this correct." Mike has a small notebook in his hand, looking over the notes he's been taking while I talk. "Two people, a man and a woman, showed up at your place in the middle of the night, demanding to be let in, and when they didn't they started to force their way inside."

"Yep." I chew and swallow another bite. "I escaped out the window and hid among a wandering pack of zombies. Then I came here."

"And you haven't contacted the police?" He taps his pen on the pad.

"No, like I said, I wasn't getting a signal at home for some reason, and then I forgot and left my phone behind." I take a sip of water to help clear my throat. "I am telling the police now, though, officer."

"Not officially. I'm just here as a friend right now." He leans back and puts his notebook on the table. "Though as soon as you are done here, that's exactly what we are going to do."

"Oh, and thanks for the safety upgrade on the front door." My fork ends up pointed straight at him. "If you hadn't done that, I wouldn't be here right now."

"You know Mike," Julie sits down with us, finally finished with her cleaning and cooking, "safe and secure is job one." Her fingers intertwine with his and he subtly pulls the hands closer to him.

The light goes off in my head. "Oh no. I'm supposed to see Terry tonight. I…I don't know if I'm up for a night out."

"If you are even questioning it, then I say don't do it." Julie and her words of wisdom.

"I'll give him a call later." My nose wrinkles. "Assuming my phone is still at my house." There is a real chance that they have totally ransacked my apartment, I suddenly realize. I'm going to get home and find out that I have nothing of value, and everything sentimental that I own will be torn up and tossed around the house.

And an hour later I couldn't have been more wrong.

Not a single thing is out of place. The front door is unlocked. The escape ladder is back in its caddy under the window. It's like nothing ever happened. I stand there in amazement as a pair of officers walk around my home before approaching me.

"Well, Ms. Cole, we can't seem to find anything out of place." According to his name badge, the officer's name is Tucker. "Can you give us any more information about the event? Did they threaten you in any way? Give any hint as to who they were?"

Dammit. "No. No, they didn't. The only thing I can give you is the names they told me, Alex and Alice."

"Well, that's not a lot to go on, you understand." I don't like the sound of this. It gets worse when Mike and the other officer walk back inside.

"We've asked around the building, but nobody heard anything last night." Mike sounds both bothered and disappointed. "I'm sorry, Cici."

"That's not possible! They were—well, she was pounding on my door. It was shaking the whole place. One of my neighbors had to hear." I would make a joke about it being loud enough to wake the dead, but…well, you understand.

"That's not what the neighbors are saying," Mike sighs. "Look, it's not like we don't believe you, Cici, it's just that we don't have anything that we can do right now."

Officer Tucker steps over beside Mike and adds his wisdom. "My advice to you is to keep the door locked tight, don't open it for anyone, and if they show back up call us immediately."

"I tried to do that last night," I mumble.

"Well, don't take any chances, Ms. Cole." I can hear the genuine concern in Tucker's voice, but can only feel frustration in what is happening. "We've got to go, but we're never more than a phone call away."

"Thank you, officers." I do mean that, even if it doesn't sound it. "I appreciate everything."

Mike looks over at me with a scowl. "I'll be right back."

I watch him walk out the front door with the other men and then turn back to look around the house. It's immaculate. Not just not destroyed, but I would almost swear it was cleaner than it was before everything happened last night. My eyes scan the room looking for something, anything, that might be wrong. Something to prove to myself that I'm not…

"You aren't crazy, Cici." Mike's words make me jump. I didn't hear him come back inside. "I believe what you said."

"How can you? I mean, there's…nothing. Not one thing to make you believe it. I'm not sure I believe it at this point."

"There is one thing. One very definite thing." His finger comes up, directed right at me. "You. I've known you for a while, and you've never been anything but perfectly honest. You're not the type to make up stories like this."

"But…but what if it's…." I don't want to say this. "What if it's me cracking. Maybe this world is finally getting to me."

"Nah. Not like this." He takes a deep breath and lets it out. "Do me a favor, and go pack a bag. I don't want you sleeping here tonight, and neither would Jules. I want you crashing with us for a night or two."

It's a tempting offer. A sensible one, too.

"I appreciate it, but I don't want to be a bother." My hand moves to my pocket, pulling free my fully-charged phone. It was nice of them to plug it in when they left. "Before I definitely say no, though, let me check something."

Fingers dance over the screen, moving through to the list of name and numbers I keep stored there. I zero in on one in particular. It rings twice before it's answered.

"Hey, Terry?" I feel my cheeks poking out and my lips spreading wide just at the mention of his name. "Can I ask a huge favor of you?"

Chapter Ten

"Thanks again for taking me in."

I've been here several times, and even slept over before, but I feel like I'm seeing Terry's place for the first time. He cleared out a drawer and some space in his closet for me, and all before I was able to gather a few things and get over here.

"Hey, don't think twice about it. It wasn't even a question." He holds out his hand, offering the glass it holds. I take it, both out of kindness and out of the hope that it actually contains whiskey. The smile on my face after one drink isn't because I took a sip of water.

"Thanks, anyway." I don't think that I sit down on the couch so much as I fall into a sitting position. I shift over as his weight pulls down the cushion a little next to me.

"I can't believe that the police aren't going to do anything." He's got a glass, too, but from the color, I don't think that it's whiskey.

"No, I understand. There is nothing for them to do. I wasn't hurt, nothing was stolen, and it didn't even look like there was a break in." My left hand reaches up and scratches my right ear.

"So...what? What happens next?" It's a good question.

"I don't know," I answer honestly. "Right now I don't really want to think about it. I'm just trying to relax and just be...not there. I've got to get some sleep tonight so I can get to work tomorrow."

"You're going to work? Really?" His eyes are suddenly huge.

"Yeah. Is that such a big surprise? Why wouldn't I?" He seems confused. "I could use the normalcy."

"Okay, yeah, but...." He's leaving a but hanging out there.

"But what?" I hate this game.

"But what if they go there?"

I blink. Several times, I'm sure. "What do you mean?"

"Those two. What if they show up to where you work?" He says that so calmly that it's distressing.

"I...I hadn't thought about that." I shake my head, clearing away the thought. "Wait, why would they? How would they even know where I work?"

"Well, they knew where you lived, didn't they?" He opens his hand palm up, as though he just revealed that idea physically.

"They just...." I close my eyes. Tightly. "Dammit. I don't want to think about that."

With an ease and amazingly soft touch, his hand comes to rest on my knee. "You need think about that kind of thing, Cici. Whoever these people are, I don't think they showed up at your place randomly."

"No, it didn't feel like that. They...they knew my name. I mean, I guess they could have gotten that information somehow, but there was something else about them. I can't put my finger on it." My body shivers and I lean over towards him. The entirety of my body melts into his as his arm wraps around my shoulder. "I don't think I've ever been that scared."

His lips touch the top of my head before he answers. "It's okay. You're safe here."

There is a long moment where the thoughts well up in my head before I finally speak. "Why?"

"Because I'm not going to let anything happen to you." It's a nice answer. Really, it is. It's just not the answer to the question I was asking.

"No. No, I mean why were they after me? I'm nobody. I don't have any money or anything. Why would they be after me?" The corners of my eyes threaten to betray me, but I'm able to hold them back for now.

"I don't know." His voice is soft and his hand equally so as he brushes back my hair. "I don't know."

The first tear rolls down my cheek, finally breaking free, and it only starts the flow. I turn my head, burying it in Terry's shoulder as the tears turn to sobs. I can't hold it back, and suddenly I don't want to. Everything comes out at once, emptying onto this poor man who's been crazy enough to take me in.

He cradles me, holding me with enough force to be reassuring without seeming oppressive. Both of my hands move up to his chest, pulled in tight between our bodies. I can feel him breathe and the beating of his heart. Calm and steady, a counter to what I'm sure is a rough erratic beat of my own.

Gradually, I turn my head up and look at him, letting our eyes meet. The smile he gives me is very different from the charming one I've seen before. There is something else in this one. A confidence and reassurance that isn't about him. Everything in his current smile is about me, and it feels wonderful.

"Do me a favor?" he asks in a soft voice. "Don't go to work tomorrow. I'm pretty sure that your boss will understand. He struck me as a nice guy."

"He is. He really is." My hand crosses over my face, wiping away what remnants I can manage from my crying jag. "I can't stay away forever, though. I want—I need that normalcy in my life."

"Well, if you want, why not come with me? I can take you to work with me. It'll give you something to take your mind off of things." His hand brushes back my hair again.

Sitting up pulls me away from his body, but I let my hands fall down from his chest towards his arms. Eventually they make their way to his hands and take a firm hold.

"Are you sure? I didn't think that the CZC allowed visitors." It's one of those secure places and most definitely not open to the public.

"Not normally, but this is unusual. I've got a little clout. As long as we keep you to certain areas, I don't think there will be a problem."

"You aren't going to get in trouble?" The last thing that I want to be is a burden, but the idea of staying with him tomorrow sounds really nice.

"I'm sure." He takes a deep breath. "I would offer to stay here with you, but there's something that I'm right in the middle of that I just can't ignore tomorrow. I might be able to pull a half day, though. We'll try to get out of there early, okay?"

And right then, suddenly it was. "Yeah. Yeah, I like the sound of that." As I take in a very deep breath the concern on my face pulls back into a smile. He's looking over at me and smiling as well, and, frankly, he's just too irresistible at that moment.

He seems more than slightly startled by the sudden lunge towards him and the kiss that follows. I give him credit, though, he recovers nicely, and is more than happy to return my affection. Last night was one of the worst experiences of my life, but this night? This night is on the complete opposite side of the pendulum. And I need it. I need him.

Tomorrow is something that I cannot control, but this moment is something that I can savor, and I'm not about to let the past or the future ruin right now for me.

Later, as I drift off to sleep in his arms, I don't let fear overtake me. I don't dream of being a fox or of deer or even of Alice and Alex. My dreams are filled from a time when life was a little simpler, and zombies were just a thing from wild stories. When my brother and I were on speaking terms, and when both of my parents were still alive.

I see my father sitting at the kitchen table, having a cup of coffee early one morning. There is a chance that he's been up all night waiting for me, but more than likely he's just getting up to go to work. My time in college was filled with many, many nights when I saw the dawn before I went to sleep, so this isn't something new. I come in giddy and silly, thrilled over the newest man in my life, sure that I know everything and have all the answers for my life. And my father rarely lectured me, at least not in the traditional sense, but I could sense that something was coming.

On this particular night—or in this particular dream, I'm not sure whether this is memory or imagination—he simply smiles and pulls out a chair for me. I'm tempted to decline and head to bed, but for some reason I sit.

"Let me just say this," he begins in that deep voice of his, "there was once a mouse who lived by the railroad tracks. She was always running back and forth across the tracks, going here and there all the time, fast as could be. One day she stopped, not realizing that she hadn't quite made it all the way across yet. The train came racing down the tracks, and it ran right over her tail, cutting off the very tip of it. She was so shocked that she turned around quickly, and in doing so put her head out onto the tracks, and the next car decapitated her, killing her instantly." He took a deep breath. "So, the moral of this? Don't ever lose your head over a little piece of tail."

I laugh, he laughs, and then I head off to bed.

I really should have listened to my father more often.

Chapter Eleven

I wanted to say something clever. Something intelligent.
You know, the type of thing that would have left an indelible
impression on Terry for the rest of his life.

What did I manage? "Wow. This place is cool."

Yeah, that is the insightful commentary that makes me feel like
I'm on the cutting edge of everything.

Of course, I am also telling the truth. The CZC is cool. Every
step I take has my head turning one way or another. I'd had my
fair share of fancy offices in the past, either working or visiting,
but this place is on a totally different level.

"Yeah, I know." The grin on Terry's face is somewhere between
pride and mutual awe. "I feel like I'm working in a lab for a
super spy organization or something."

My laugh almost drowns out my reply. "So long as it isn't the
evil villain organization."

"Nah. If we were the evil villain organization the management
would let cats into the place." He looks over at me and shakes
his head. "I checked. The boss doesn't have any cats."

Sounds like a valid argument. We head towards a large desk, and the obvious security people who are sitting behind it. Past them is a huge wall of frosted glass, spanning one hundred feet wide, easily, and standing probably twenty or so feet high. There are two large doors in the wall, also glass, one on either side of the desk. The desk itself seems to be made of a combination of steel and glass, and is about twenty feet wide. Four security people—all men—nod as we get closer.

"Morning, Carl." Terry gives a slight wave and nod to the man on the left side of the desk. "Gonna need a visitor badge."

The man—Carl, I assume—grabs a clip board and flips through the first few pages. "I'm not seeing anything on here about a guest today, Mr. Stone. Did you submit the paperwork?"

"No, I didn't." He winces. Terry warned me that this might be a bit of a challenge on the drive over. He made it sound much more certain last night. I'm guessing because he didn't want me saying no to him—which I would have done, actually, so it was a good ploy on his part. "Any chance on getting it pushed through?"

"I can't clear it, Mr. Stone. You'll have to get permission from higher up." Carl reaches for the phone and picks up the receiver. "You want me to place a call?"

Instead of answering, Terry turns to me and takes a deep breath. As he does so, his lips get very thin. "I'm going to need you to stay here, Cici. I'll just be a few minutes. I've got to go in and talk to some people before I can get you past this point." He tries to turn those lips into a smile. "Okay?"

Turning my head in a slow arc, I eventually bring my gaze back to him. "It's not like I have a lot of choices." I try to smile, too. I'm guessing it's about as convincing as the one he gave me.

He gestures to the other side of the room and the several large chairs and couches that sit beside the windows. "Go have a seat. I won't be long."

After I give him a nod, he walks to the door on the left side of the desk, passes his ID card in front of the sensor next to it, and opens the door. For a brief moment I see beyond to a second door, also glass, though this one clear, and what appears to be a large gathering of tables beyond. From the split second view I got, they don't appear to be desks or cubicles, but more elevated tables of some kind.

My eyes shift over to Carl, who is staring at me. I'm not sure if he's trying to be stoic, intimidating, or just casual, but whichever it is, he needs to work on it. I give him the awkward smile and gesture vaguely towards the furniture.

A couple dozen steps later and I'm there. Like the rest of the place, the furniture is impressive. White leather and steel, with what looks to be walnut accents, but I'm really not that good with identifying types of wood. It's not too extreme to guess that one of the chairs alone probably costs two months of my current salary. It's the type of furniture that always makes me feel a little uncomfortable about the idea of actually sitting on it, so I choose to stand.

Which actually, isn't that bad.

The panorama beyond the furniture is enough to take my breath away. Some would probably call it a garden, but to me it is more of a sculpture or a display. Most, though, would likely just call it a waterfall. The only problem with that is the fact that there is nothing for the water to fall off of—it just falls.

Imagine a sheet of water, falling from nowhere down into a basin below. If you can do that, you can see the waterfall outside the main lobby of the CZC. Standing what I would guess to be about twenty feet high, and easily a hundred feet long—probably to mimic the glass display behind me—a solid wall of water falls down from the air. It's not falling off of anything, it simply falls. For the life of me, I have no idea how they make it happen. It looks like magic, but I know that isn't the case, so all I can do is wonder and let my brain try to look past the impossible and find the possible. I feel like I could stare at it for hours, getting lost in its mystery.

"Impressive, isn't it?"

I'm pretty sure I jump about a foot into the air. There is no doubt that my heart stops completely for a few seconds. When the rest of me finally establishes that I'm definitely going to live, my heart rejoins me and I look over at the source of the voice.

At first, I see an old man, but a moment later I also see my mistake. On second glance, I'd put him at forty, or maybe a little above that, but not much. There are touches of grey in his hair, yes, but the majority of it is still dark brown. And he is smallish, maybe two or three inches shorter than me, but it's deep within the caverns of his eyes where his age becomes an illusion. Lines become crags, dragging your eyes in towards his own, where it seems that only darkness dwells. Despite that rather dismal description, he is wearing a smile and his voice is soft.

"Sorry, I didn't mean to startle you," he half laughs.

"It's okay. It's okay." I let my breath catch up to my words. "I let myself get that distracted. Not your fault."

"Still, it is impressive." He looks away from me and back to the waterfall.

"Yeah, very. I have no idea how that thing can do that." Don't get too technical with your description, Cici.

Another half laugh puts him to a total of one full one so far. "Well, it is a pretty impressive trick." He leans over slightly towards me, still keeping his eyes on the outside. "If you want the illusion ruined, I can tell you the secret."

"Huh." Not the most coherent of answers, but it matches my mood.

"Do you want me to tell you?" He glances my way so I look back.

"I don't know." I take a deep breath, giving myself a moment. "I mean, I'm very curious, but, like you said, that would ruin the illusion. Take away the mystery of it. Part of me wants that mystery to stick around until I figure it out or just accept it as unexplainable." My head shifts to the left. "The other part of me, though, is just dying to know the truth, so I don't have to spend any more time wondering about the darn thing."

"And which part is winning?" He raises an eyebrow, letting a little more light in towards his eye, revealing brown in the shadow that seemed to swallow the color before.

"I'm not sure." I give him a smile of my own.

He turns his head slightly. "I'm guessing you're here to meet someone?"

"Kinda. My boyfriend works here." Boyfriend? Where the hell did that word come from? "He's in the back doing something, and I get to wait for him here. You?"

"Oh, I'm just escaping the tedium of another meeting for a few minutes." He glances back at the desk and I follow briefly. Everyone there is staring at him. "I'm just visiting, too, but I get to sit in on all the meetings. You're the lucky one."

"Yeah, I can't argue with that. Meetings are their own unique form of hell." I see him again in a new light. He doesn't seem as old, but he still looks fragile. Like leaves waiting for a wind to carry them off or something.

"And I suppose I should get back. Don't want them sending out a search party." This time it's closer to a full laugh. "Made your mind up?" He nods towards the waterfall.

A smile and a nod gives him a hint, but I go ahead with the full answer. "Think I'll keep it a mystery for now. Try to chew on it for a bit."

He gives me a nod back. I'd like to think it was one of approval. "Fair enough. You have a good day. Hope your boyfriend isn't too long."

"Thanks. Hope you have a good—or at least a quick—meeting," I reply.

"Oh, I doubt it. Too many opinions never make something quick or easy, just complicated." His words drag the light away and make him old again. Without saying anything else, he turns and walks back. I watch as two of the security guards step out and open the doors for him—the ones on the right side of the desk—and he disappears behind the wall of frosted glass.

For some reason I stare after him for a minute or two. I have no idea why, and nothing happens, but I feel the need to watch, just in case. Eventually, I go back to my mystery waterfall, trying to see beyond the illusion once again. All I see is water falling down with no explanation.

And for a second time that day I let myself get caught up in it.

"Hey." This time I don't jump. I'd like to think that it was because I was more secure, but it's likely more because I recognize the voice.

"Hey." I smile as Terry walks up to me. "How'd it go?"

"Took a minute, as you can tell, but I was able to get the right clearance. You'll be able to come back with me to the main office, but you won't be able to go back to the labs where I work. Is that going to be okay?" He winces as he tells me this. I'm guessing he's afraid I'm going to be angry. I'm not sure why.

"That's fine. I don't want to be a burden, anyway." I nod back behind me at the outside. "Heck, I'd almost be willing to stay out here if I had to. It's a spectacular view."

He looks past me and his face scrunches slightly. "That? It's just a fake waterfall."

My mouth opens to say something that matches the confusion running through my mind, but all that comes out is, "Yeah, I guess."

"Come on, they're getting your badge ready. We should be able to go back in a couple of minutes. I'll introduce you around." His hand goes out, palm up, waiting for me to take it.

I look at it for a second, not really considering anything more than just looking at the offer. It only takes another second for me to put my hand in his. Together we walk over to the security desk and wait for them to finish their preparation to let me past the doors and the glass wall.

True to their word, they hand me a large badge with a clip on the back. It's heavier than it looks, likely because there are electronics built into it, I'm assuming. It's quickly explained that I have to keep it on me at all times, and that if I were to lose it for any reason, I would have to report it immediately, and yada, yada, yada. There might have been something important in all of that, but Carl wasn't exactly the most captivating speaker. Instead, I turn and walk over to the left-hand doors that I saw Terry go through earlier, and he's right beside me. He opens the door, and I step through it in front of him.

And thus began my first day at the CZC.

Chapter Twelve

I hate going to parties where I only know one person. It's not that I'm antisocial or anything, it's just that, to me, it seems parties devolve into cliques of people hanging out together and chatting about old times. And if you only know one person you want to hang out with them, but you don't fit in with everyone else.

Sure, sometimes you make new friends and have a great time and everything goes perfect, but more often than not it seems that I'm always left standing around with a drink in my hand smiling politely at stories that have obvious meaning to everyone listening to them but me. I have no point of reference.

So, welcome to the CZC.

I got to see what was hinted at behind the glass doors, and it didn't disappoint. Several rows of high tables with chairs around them, obviously meant for meetings or discussions or some other form of get-together, only placed square in the middle of the room, so not exactly a place for private meetings.

Like the lobby, this room is the model of modern design aesthetic. I had no idea that the CZC both made that kind of money and that they were willing to spend it on superficial design elements. I'm not complaining mind you, it's just rather surprising.

Oh, and in addition to the high tables, there are several work stations in what I would call an open-cube layout. Meaning they are still in the grid pattern that you see in the average cube farm office, but they don't have the walls separating them. It's a very open, inviting layout.

Of course there is also no one sitting at them. At least not in the time that I've been here. I did see one woman come by and open a drawer on a desk and pull something out. It might have been lunch, or it might have been a key component in something she was working on in the back rooms, I can't be sure. She isn't one of the people that I've met so far today. Those people would be Greg, Thomas—not Tom, but Thomas, he made that clear—Nicole, James, and Isaiah.

I, on the other hand, have been given my own special space. I call it "The Chair." Mostly because it's a chair. Granted, it's a pretty nice, very comfy chair, but that's really all it is. I can see some people from The Chair through the next layer of glass walls—there is a lot of glass in this place—but I can't hear a thing. I've taken to adding in my own conversation to what I'm seeing. For instance, currently there is a debate on whether or not you can actually convert sea water into salt water taffy directly that is being held between three people. The two men are holding onto their staunch belief that it is chemically impossible for this transformation to occur, but the woman involved keeps referencing the magic candy stone, and the amazing power it has to physically transmute anything. The two men are skeptics, but she feels that the candy stone has the power to turn even their jaded hearts into a delicious caramel that will warm them throughout.

It is entirely possible that I'm completely wrong about their conversation, though.

"Hey, Cici."

Terry's voice draws my attention away from my personally subtitled play and back to the room I'm in, in a not-too-jarring manner. I suddenly realize that I'm sitting sideways in what I'm sure is a very expensive chair, and hasten to straighten up—especially when I see that Terry isn't alone.

Popping up from The Chair, I half expect a hug or a peck on the cheek when Terry gets close, but instead he stops just shy of physical contact.

"Cici, I want you to meet a couple of people. This is Roger," he indicates a grey-haired gentleman, who extends his hand, which I meet for a polite shake, "and this is Demarius." A tall, rather dashing-looking man with dark brown skin also extends his hand, which again I meet.

"So, you're the zombie whisperer, eh?" Demarius asks.

"I…beg your pardon?" I'm guessing that my eyes are different sizes at the moment.

"It's, uh, sort of a joke," Terry scratches the back of his head and avoids looking at me.

"Terry has been bragging about you and your encounter with the zombie at your F.O.O.D.Z. station. He claims that you were able to alter their feeding habits." Roger has a smooth, easy voice. The type you like to associate with your father—though mine sounded nothing like that.

"Well, yeah, basically, I guess. I just gave them new food." I shrug.

"Do you mind if we talk to you about it?" Roger asks.

"No. No, that would be great, actually. It'd make me feel like I was doing something other than warming The Chair." I send a vague gesture towards the seat behind me.

"Well, then let's go sit in a different set of chairs." Roger steps aside, and Demarius laughs lightly. Taking the cue, I move over towards the raised tables, expecting to get some direction as I get closer. When I hear only silence, I eventually stop and turn back towards them. Terry is right behind me and gently puts his arm on my back and walks towards a particular table.

"Over here," he says just loud enough for me to hear. "Sorry about this."

"No worries! I wasn't kidding about it giving me something to do," I say in earnest.

Walking to the far side of the table, I take the first seat that I find. Terry moves just past my chair, sitting down beside me, while Roger and Demarius sit across from us. The table isn't too wide, maybe just over two feet, giving it a surprisingly intimate feeling.

"You want to go over what happened?" Roger asks.

"Uh, sure." And so I go into the story—again. Seeing Curly. Zombies stop eating cabbage. Seeing Curly again. Going out to see him with cabbage. No go. Getting cereal. Giving cereal. Getting a good response. Yay, cereal-eating zombies. The end.

"Can you detail the behavior you saw in this one zombie? The one you call Curly?" The look in Demarius' eyes is just above intense, but still one notch down from creepy.

"Well, like I said, I saw him holding up the cabbage. Like he was showing it off." Please don't make me repeat the whole story in question-sized snippets.

"No, no, I'm sorry. I wasn't clear. I meant when you went out and confronted him," Demarius explains.

"Oh!" Okay, better question. "Yeah, um, well, I don't…I don't know. I'm not sure how I would describe his behavior. I just went out there, got his attention, and tried to give him the cabbage, and—"

"How did you get his attention?" Roger breaks in before I can finish.

"I threw a cabbage at him." I don't think that's the answer he was looking for, but that's what I did.

"And he didn't attack you? Didn't see that as provocation?" Demarius asks.

"He didn't attack me, so no, I guess not."

"What sort of reaction did he have?"

I think back. It's been a while, so I do what I can to remember the details. "He was…confused? Like he didn't understand what I was doing. Or he was annoyed. I think I remember that, anyway."

"It's very important that you remember, Cici," Roger states. "Was he annoyed with you?"

My mind goes back. I remember one eye and a hole in his neck. And that he wasn't too decayed just yet, but still reeked to high heaven. His head lolled over to one side. "No. No, he wasn't annoyed. He was…I think he was curious, actually."

Both men sit up a little higher and fidget in their seats.

"Okay, okay. Now, how did you get him to eat the cereal? What did you do?" The tone of Demarius' voice has clearly gone up an octave, and the words are coming much faster now.

"I tore open the box and took a bite. Just like I said," I answer.

"Yeah but…but…." Demarius can't get the words out.

"Did you do anything else? Say anything? Make any kind of gesture?" Roger is kind enough to finish the question for him.

My hand comes to my chin to help my brain process thoughts. That's the only explanation for why I scratch my chin when I'm thinking, so I'm sticking to it. "I guess I did. I seem to recall telling him something. Trying to convince him that the corn flakes were really good or flavorful or…I don't know." I try to picture myself on the grounds that day. "Oh, and I made a few gestures with my hand, like I was showing him how to eat. I don't know why, it's clear that he knew how to eat."

They both sit up and look at each other. You would swear by appearances that they were nine-year-olds who were just told they were going to Disneyworld. It is very obvious they are doing everything they can to not just start laughing themselves silly. Eventually, they do turn back to look at me.

"Thank you! Thank you so much!" Demarius says as he reaches across to shake my hand again. I oblige.

"You've helped us more than you know," Roger adds on. "Please excuse us, we've got to go back and…. Well, we've got to go into the back."

"No problem. Glad I could help." I'm sure I sounded just as confused as much as anything else.

"It was a true delight meeting you." For a second I think that Demarius is going to try to shake my hand again.

"Yes, wonderful," Roger says as he grabs Demarius by the arm. "Thank you so much, again."

And then they scampered off, passing through another security checkpoint and going into the next level of…whatever it is that makes up the levels of this place.

"Well, that was certainly exciting. For them at least," I laugh to Terry. He's got a big grin on his face.

"They were dying to meet you. I'd been telling them pretty much the exact same thing that you said, almost word-for-word in some cases, but I think they thought I was just trying to make myself look good or something." He leans in, resting on the table and looking up at me with that damn smile of his. "Thanks."

"I don't know what I did, but you're welcome." I find myself leaning a little towards him, as well. For a moment it's easy to forget where we are, and, thankfully, I've almost totally forgotten the entire reason that I'm here today—until just now when I reminded myself, anyway.

"Bo!"

It's one word, spoken loudly from the doorway without being shout, but it's enough to cause Terry to jerk his head around quickly.

"Now?" he asks.

There is a man I've never seen before standing in the previously mentioned doorway. "Yep, and seemingly on a warpath."

"Dammit!" Terry gets up from his chair and pushes it back into place. I suddenly feel the need to do the exact same thing.

"Something wrong?" I ask.

"No, not really. Just my boss." He looks at me and opens his eyes wide. "My big boss. The one two steps above my boss, actually."

"Oh! Okay, so what…" I look around the room, "…what do I need to do?"

He shakes his head. "Nothing. Just go back to sitting. Sorry." He actually looks a little pained to say that.

"No problem. I'll be fine." I take the chance and lean over and give him a little peck on the cheek. I'd swear that he blushes afterwards.

"Okay. Well, I gotta go to the back. I don't want to be seen as lazy." He's already walking away before I can say anything.

"You go. Be busy and don't get in trouble." I laugh and give him a little wave.

Once more I'm alone. Just me and The Chair, ready to renew our relationship. I come up to it and greet it in our old familiar way of not saying anything to each other, and sit down. Naturally, my head goes around to looking through the glass and I'm stunned to see dramatic developments in the ongoing saga I've been watching. A fourth person—I can only assume a long-lost sibling—has appeared. It seems that he has taken the side of our heroine, and is ready to defend her honor and the honor of the candy stone against the men who would besmirch it.

Sadly, I don't get to witness the next stage in the storyline. A door opens on the far side of the room, and it's a door I've seen no one else use so far. Through it steps a woman who will not be easily overlooked. If you don't notice her height or the breadth of her shoulders, you will still be sucked in by her aura. Her dark hair is pulled tightly back and seems to head down well past her shoulders, and her eyes are just as dark. I hesitate to call her pretty, but she's far from unattractive. Handsome would be the word I would use for her, I think. I glance at her shoes—yes, I look at people's shoes, sue me—and notice she's wearing flats, which only makes my eyes go a little wider. She'd be terrifying in a pair of heels—that is, if she wasn't already.

And she's walking directly towards me.

All I can do is shift uneasily in The Chair, waiting for her to come up on me. Suddenly, images of the two people outside my door rush over me and I'm feeling trapped again. My eyes dart around the room looking for an exit strategy, but before I can develop anything she's standing in front of me, staring down. The world retracts and I become a little child standing before the principal at school.

"Ms. Cole?" Her voice is surprisingly soft. My only answer to it is a blink. "You are Cassandra Cole, correct?"

I think I nod. I must have done something, because she smiles at me.

"My name is Deborah Dunn. I'm the chief agent for the southeast quadrant of the Federal Office of Organizing Dining for Zombies." She takes a step back. "You might have heard someone calling out an alert for 'Bo.' That's me."

"Oh." I shift around and finally find enough footing to stand up. I extend my hand towards her. "It's a pleasure to meet you. And yes, I'm Cassandra Cole." She takes my hand, and as I guessed, has a rather firm grip.

"It's a pleasure to meet you Ms. Cole." She gives me a smile, and her features soften. They don't go soft—not by any measure, actually—but they do soften.

"I haven't gotten Terry—um, that is Terry Stone—in trouble, have I? I'm trying to stay out of the way here." A thought occurs to me. "Or have I gotten in trouble? Am I in trouble?"

She laughs gently. "Not at all, Ms. Cole. Quite the opposite, actually." Her smile changes slightly. "In fact, I'm here to offer you a job."

Huh. Well, I didn't see that coming.

Chapter Thirteen

"You're kidding, right?"

"Not even a little bit." It's hard to hide my smile, though I do my very best.

"I don't believe it, still." Terry is shaking his head. I know he is shaking his head, because that's what he's been doing ever since I saw him after the offer came down earlier today.

"Hey, I'm proud of you, Cici." Julie's husband, Mike, is pretty much beaming. "I'm also not a bit surprised. I know how smart you are, and obviously this woman saw the same thing. What was her name again?"

"Deborah," I answer, "though I kinda want to call her Didi."

"No. No, no, no." The familiar chime of a fork setting down abruptly onto a china plate rises from the table, and we all turn to Terry who is raising up both hands. "Please, whatever you do, don't call her that." Both of his index fingers were wavering in the air as he speaks. "Seriously, she's not long on a sense of humor."

"I don't know, she seemed nice during our talk." I shrug.

"That's another thing," he grabs his glass of wine up and takes a long sip, "how long did she talk to you?"

"Not long. Maybe fifteen minutes?" I put a bite of Julie's famous pot roast in my mouth. I really wish that my mom had taught me to cook this well.

"Yeah, I'm not buying it." He picked up his fork again and went back to work on his dinner.

"What is your problem, man?" Mike asks with a laugh. "Don't you want her working there with you?"

"Well, I'm not sure she's going to be working directly with me. Did Bo tell you what your duty was going to be yet?" Terry's gone fully into detective mode it seems.

"Not yet. I'm meeting her Monday morning to go over everything. She said that she has to push the paperwork through before anything can go further. I guess I'll find out then."

Julie is almost glowing. As soon as I called and told her about the job offer she told me—didn't invite me, but told me—that Terry and I were coming over for dinner tonight. "This is so great."

"We don't even know if I'll like the job, Julie. I'm not going to make a judgment call just yet."

"What do you mean?" Her eyes bug out at me. "You're going to be getting away from the zombies, at least directly. You're going to be getting a pay raise. And you get to got to work with your man. What's not to love?"

Okay, so maybe I'm almost as excited as she is about this whole thing. "Let's not get carried away."

"No, she's right," Mike adds. "Getting away from the feeding hub is a good thing. Just about every outbreak of violence has happened around those things. The further you are away from them, the better."

"Yeah, but she could end up hating working with me. Work and relationships can be a bad combination sometimes."

Oh. I hear it in Terry's voice for the first time. That nagging little sound that crawls up the back of your neck and gnaws on you a little bit at a time. Fear.

"Hey." I reach over and put my hand on his arm. "Work won't change things between us. Or, if it does, I'm guessing it'll only be for the better."

Our eyes met, and I saw something deeper in his for the first time. The warmth of his hand covers over mine, and I feel the firm grasp of his fingers. His mouth moves, not quite forming words despite his initial effort. There is a bit of a long silence in the room immediately after—at least until Mike breaks it up.

"Okay, Terry!" He stands and grabs his plate and then reaches over in front of Julie and picks her's up as well. "The women cooked, so we get to clean. Standard rules."

His hand leaves my arm and I see him point at me. "She didn't cook anything!"

"She's the special guest at this dinner. She gets special treatment." Mike laughs, Terry joins him, and then we all join in. "Now pick up a plate and let's get to cleaning!"

There is a clear reluctance in Terry even as he acquiesces and picks up both my plate and his. It's not a surprise that my eyes are on him as he walks away towards the kitchen, but it is a little bit of a curiosity to see Julie's eyes going there, too.

"So," she turns back to look at me with a grin that could split her head in two, "what's it like?"

"Uh…." What? Is this high school again? "Not sure I'm following you."

"Living with him! You've been there two days now. How's it going?"

"Oh!" Yeah, that makes more sense. "It's, uh, well, it's okay, I guess. Not really sure. It's only been two days."

"Yeah, but you have an idea, right? You can tell." She gets up and moves to the chair next to mine, lowering her voice as she does. "It's like when Mike and I went on our first vacation together. That was when I knew I could marry him. Once you're forced to spend time sequestered with someone, you get a real feeling for whether or not you'd be able to spend your life with them."

Alert! Alert! Friend going too far! Throw up a towel and call for a signal or something like that!

"It's only been two days, Jules. Don't you think it's a bit too early to even think about the whole marriage idea?"

"Marriage?" Her head actually recoils enough that her neck disappears. "I'm not talking about you getting married."

A quick head count for the room confirms that she and I are the only ones currently present. Just wanted to make sure. "Then who was it that was just talking about spending time together and discovering that you were marriage compatible?"

"No, no. I was just using that as a comparison. You guys haven't spent nearly enough time together to think about marriage. I'm just talking about looking at it as, you know, a more relationshippy kind of relationship."

"I have no idea what that even means." Sure, tell yourself that. You're the one who used the word "boyfriend" so casually today. You're not supposed to have a boyfriend, dummy. You told yourself that you weren't going to do that because the world is going to hell and there is no point, remember?

"It means that you have someone. Someone who is there for you when you need them. Someone that you can trust and count on." Dammit, Jules, don't get so damn romantic on me, it's contagious.

"Hey, I like him. Isn't that enough?" Keep saying it, Cici.

"Sure, but deep down, don't you want more than just someone you like?" And there we have it. Julie is staring straight into me, trying to pull out that other person she keeps trying to find.

"Look, Julie, I…I don't know. I like Terry—really, I do—but I still have issues about getting serious with anyone right now. Does it have to be like that? Can't I just have a casual thing going?"

Some of the light dims from her face. "Of course you can, honey, but I just…" She takes a deep breath and the sigh that comes out says more than her words. "Just don't miss out on something because you're being stubborn."

I laugh. Openly and out loud. There is no explanation as to why, but I do it anyway.

"I'll tell you what. I'm about to start working with this guy. If we can survive that—and that is normally a very big if—then I'll start looking at this as a more serious option, okay?" I take a deep breath and hold mine. Hopefully, Julie won't take too long to answer me.

"Okay," she replies, and I let my breath out, happily. She then settles back a little in her chair. "So, tell me more about this job. What are you going to be doing? Are you going to be working directly with Terry? What is his job anyway?"

Don't hold back, Jules. Go ahead and ask all of your questions at once, why don't you? "Well, like I said earlier, I don't know what my job is going to be, so I don't know whether or not I'll be working with Terry, and…." My face probably contorts oddly based on how I feel. "Actually, I have no idea what Terry does there. He's never told me."

"Really? So, he still hasn't told you? I wonder if that means that you won't be able to talk to me about work, either?" Something somewhere between frown and pout appears on Julie's face.

"I have no idea. Maybe." I shrug. "I do know that they have some tight security. Just visiting there was a challenge. I had to stay in the lobby for a long time." Light comes on. "Oh! Did I tell you about the waterfall?"

"What waterfall?"

I give her a smile. "I'll take that as a 'no.' Just outside the lobby—which is an impressive thing on its own, let me tell you—there is this huge waterfall. That would be cool enough, except that this waterfall seems to fall out of nowhere. It just… is."

"What do you mean?"

"It's like it just falls out of the air. About, oh, I think it was about twenty feet high and it had to be a hundred feet long, and it just falls. There is nothing, and then there is a waterfall." I feel myself get a little higher in my chair.

"What? How? Where does it come from?" Julie sits up, too, matching me giddy for giddy.

"I don't know! I'm working on it, though. The guy I met said that it was actually a pretty simple explanation once you figure it out. He even offered to tell me, but I told him that I wanted to figure it out for myself." Which has me immediately going through things that could do it, ranging from magic to…well, right now I'm stuck on magic, to be honest.

"What guy?" We both turn to see Terry walk in with a dish rag.

"I don't know. I didn't ask his name. Some guy that was there for some sort of conference or something." I watch Terry tuck the rag in his belt and then pick up a couple more plates that need washing.

"Conference?" His eyes narrow and I can see the wheels start to turn in his mind. "I don't know any conference going on." He pauses for a beat. "What did he look like?"

"Middle age. Brown hair with some grey. A little shorter than me." To help clarify, I hold my hand out beside me standing slightly below my head level, because that's how tall he would be if he was standing next to me while I was seated.

Terry's face changes. At first it's that proverbial light going off moment, but after that it just goes…blank.

"Interesting. I don't know who that is." Huh. Okay…. "What did he say to you?"

"Not much. We just talked about the waterfall. He said he was trying to escape a meeting of some sort for a few minutes and just wandered into the lobby." I twist my head to the side, giving me a better perspective on asking a question. Why else would I do that? "Are you sure you don't know him?"

"Nope. Have no idea who that is." He quickly stands up and turns away. "More dishes to clean!" And with that he hurries out of the room.

Something remains lingering in the room after him, but Julie's next words tell me I'm the only one who notices. "So, did you figure out what causes the waterfall? Are there people doing magic at the CZC?"

My head comes around to look at her and my mouth opens up ready to answer, but I can't find the words right away. It takes more than a moment for them to find their way from my head to my mouth.

"I don't know," I answer. "I wouldn't put anything past a possibility right now."

Chapter Fourteen

"Thank you so much for coming in today."

Her smile is warm, her hand is extended, and the chair is already pulled out for me. Everything seems perfect, which is probably one of the reasons I'm scared half to death.

"Shouldn't I be saying that to you?" Okay, I think that was a little loud. And a little laugh-y. And…oh crap, just don't think about it.

"Actually, no. I am truly grateful. You could have easily said no." Her grip is firm, just like before, and immediately after releasing my hand she gestures to the chair.

"Well, it seems like the opportunity of a lifetime. I would have been an idiot to say no to you." The chair isn't as comfortable as I would expect, and I squirm a little more than I would like.

"You could still have easily said no, so, again, thank you." Deborah—Bo, Didi, or whatever I'm supposed to call her, Ms. Dunn, I suppose, actually—settles back and gives me a long casual look. Which makes me shift in the chair again. "Did everything go okay with HR this morning? They get all of your paperwork done?"

"I think so. It was a lot of paperwork, so I hope so." I think I signed my name forty times this morning.

"Well, we are a secure building, so there are a lot of issues that are particular to us. Which is one of the reasons that we're having this conversation—I want to make sure you understand our unique situation here at the CZC."

"The nice man in HR went over that with me already, but I'd love to hear your take on it, too." First lie. The man in HR—Brian, Brad, Brozilla, it was something like that—pretty much hammered into my head that everything I saw and/or did here was top secret and I couldn't so much as talk about it outside these walls or I would be thrown in jail and have my car, house, life, and dog—or future dog in my case, since currently I don't have one—taken away from me.

"Well, I'm sure that Brock went over everything in detail, so I won't hit those spots again," oh, thank God, "but I do want to talk about what we do here, and why it's important. What do you know about the CZC?"

"Well, it's the Center for Zombie Control, and it's considered the country's, and maybe the world's, leading facility for zombie research." Which I think is what is says on the promotional tour pamphlet.

"And that's it?" She raises an eyebrow and I suddenly feel stupid.

"Uh, yeah. But that's a good thing, right? It means that your security is working the way that it's supposed to." Spin it round, sister!

She laughs, and the muscles in my neck have a half-ton taken off of them.

"I suppose. Since you're here with us now, though, I think that you might want a few more details." There is a deep breath before she starts talking. I think its from both of us. "When the zombies first appeared, everything in the world went into an instant state of chaos, as I'm sure you remember. The idea that we were finally experiencing a true end-of-the-world scenario became far too real. Hundreds of thousands of people, if not more, lost their lives, and mostly from the human response and not the actual zombies. You may be surprised to hear how small the mortality rate from zombies actually is, to be honest

"That does not, however, reduce the risk presented by them. The sheer number of lifeless lifeforms is already on the verge of outnumbering the living. In only a few years, we will see the balance of this world shift from living to unliving as the most numerous human life on Earth.

"To that end, we here at the CZC are working two-fold to prevent that from happening. We are first trying to find the cause for the creation of the zombies. What brought them up out of the grave to begin with, and what might be done to reverse that and end this nightmare for everyone."

That first deep breath comes to completion and she takes a moment to gather in a second one.

"The second issue we must address is developing a way to destroy the zombies utterly if we are unable to reverse the plague that has beset us. Currently, the only means that we have to destroy them is so severe that it is a genuine risk to the living as well as the unliving.

"As I'm sure you are aware, steps have been taken to help prevent the further spread of the zombie plague, chief of which is the fact that anyone who dies today will have their remains cremated within an hour by law, and even then it is sometimes not fast enough."

"Why is that?" My mouth moves faster than my mind can stop it.

"Good question." I'm so glad she said that. "Unfortunately, why the dead rise at different rates is one of the things that we haven't figured out just yet. That falls into the first of the two categories that we have: trying to figure out what's bringing the dead back to life—or unlife, as the case may be."

"Oh, yeah. That makes sense." Hopefully my smile looks confident and not embarrassed.

"To my point, however, the work that we do here must be kept in total secrecy. Not because we are trying to keep it from anyone, but because letting it out could create false rumors and even more panic. Our world is hanging in a very precarious position, and as a part of our team you will be fighting to turn that balance back towards the living. Back towards hope."

It's at about this point that I want to stand up and cheer, volunteering to go to the front lines and defend our world from these damn creatures. The woman knows how to give a speech.

Fortunately, there is another thought more pressing on my mind. "So, if I may ask—and not to sound ungrateful—but, why are you wanting me to work here? I mean, I'm not exactly qualified for scientific research."

Her light laugh eases my nerves a little bit and helps me stare this gift horse directly in the mouth. "Not everyone here is a scientist, Ms. Cole. I'm not. I was brought here because of my management and administrative abilities. I assure you that we have special plans for you."

"That…sounds kind of ominous, actually." I quickly check her lap for a fluffy white cat, despite what Terry already told me. She's clear. It looks like I'm safe.

"It wasn't meant to. In fact, it was meant as a compliment." She stands up and steps around her desk. I'm not sure whether to stay seated and stare up at her or stand—and stare up at her. "The story of what happened with you and the zombies at your facility has created quite the stir around here."

"Really?" How many people has Terry told about me?

"Indeed. It's why I'm putting you on the behavioral team." She motions her arm out towards the door. "Walk with me, please."

The chair slides away quickly as I pop up next to her, and instead of going ahead and moving forward, I stand still, waiting for her to take the first step. As she does, I move right along with her.

"You see, Ms. Cole, the idea of altering the eating habits of the zombies has been something that we have been working on for years. If we can control what they eat, then they pose less and less of a threat. Some even feel that we could effectively neutralize them if we become the ones in control of their habits."

"I'm still not sure how I fit in to that," I answer honestly. "I mean, yes, I did do that. Once. And I basically got lucky."

"I don't believe in luck, Ms. Cole." She turns her head and looks at me and I feel thirteen suddenly. "Work and intelligence is what achieves results."

"I've got one of those," I laugh. "Oh, and please, call me Cici. Everyone does."

"Nothing personal, Ms. Cole, but I like to keep things on a professional level." There is no anger or malice in her voice, just a casual disregard. I would have preferred the anger or malice.

"Oh, okay."

"As I was saying, you will be working on the behavioral research team, helping us to find out if you can replicate what you did with the zombies back at your previous position." A smile leads into her next words. "And to help you out, that also means you'll be working with Mr. Stone."

"Terry? He works in that department?" It's the first hint I've had at what he actually does.

"He does indeed. In fact, he's one of the better behavioral scientists that we have. The work that he's done with our zombies has been exceptional." We turn and are suddenly in a huge hallway with walls of frosted glass on either side. Several doors are littered along either side of the passage at various intervals.

"Huh." Again with my witty banter.

"He hadn't told you about that?" One of her eyebrows elevates slightly.

"No, he's been a good boy. He hasn't given up any secrets." A memory runs through my head and it causes a chuckle. "Except of course that he hates pizza."

Her gait slows down, all but coming to a stop. "I beg your pardon?"

"Oh, um, it's just that he talks in his sleep sometimes and he's mumbled about pizza several times. Each time he sounds a little stressed when he does." I swallow down the elephant that is hanging in my throat. "When I asked him about it, he said that he doesn't like pizza."

"Really? I didn't know that about him. I'll certainly remember that."

Our pace picks back up as we continue down the hallway. "Well, you don't want to get to know your employees on a personal level, so that's not the type of thing that you're really going to find out otherwise." Oh God, did I just say that? Why did I say that?

Fortunately, she only smiles. "You raise a good point."

We stop and she turns, facing me. "We're here." Her hand motions vaguely to the door on her right. It looks like all the other doors, except that it has "Laboratory GG" on it. "You go on inside and find Mr. Stone. He'll give you a tour of the lab and take you to your desk." Her hand extends and I take it, getting that same firm greeting—or farewell, in this case. "Thank you again for joining us here at the CZC. I'm expecting some big things from you, Ms. Cole."

"Ooookay." How do you respond to that? "I'll…do my best."

"That's all anyone can ask. Good luck." And with that she turns and walks away, heading back the way that we came. I watch her walk maybe fifteen feet before she turns back around. "Oh, and Ms. Cole?"

"Yes?"

"If you have no other plans, stop by my office tomorrow around noon. I want to take you to lunch." I'm not sure if that was a request or a demand.

"Sure." How could I say no?

"Excellent. Go on in. I'm sure Mr. Stone is waiting."

Once again she turns away, leaving me alone in the hall. I stare over at the door and do my best to cypher the reason behind "Laboratory GG," coming up with all manner of nonsensical words that fit. Green grapefruit. Golden graduates. Goblin gobblers. Finally, I decide that it's probably just the next one in line, alphabetically, which takes off a bit of the mystique. I kinda want there to be something going on in this lab that is bizarre and extreme.

And as I reach for the handle I mentally slap myself for even thinking about that, but it was already too late.

Chapter Fifteen

"So, have you got all this?"

His smile still gets me, and he's added a touch of sweetness to it this time. The way that he's been making sure that I understood the computer system and my login and everything has been all but doting—and borderline offensive, honestly.

"Yeah, I think I know how to use a computer." I actually stick my tongue out at him. He deserves it.

"I know that! I'm just…well, I'm helping! Stop it." It's nice to see him flustered.

"Sorry. Don't mean to pick on you that way." I look away from him and back to the computer screen. Big field of blue with only three visible folders on the desktop. Before I'm done it will look like a hard drive exploded all over the damn thing, knowing the way I tend to organize files. "Okay, so is there anything else here?"

"Not according to you."

That earns a slow turn of my head until I see him and then an even slower raised eyebrow. "It's going to be like that, eh?"

"Oh hell no!" Both hands move up into the defensive position. Smart man. "I concede. And no, that pretty much covers the whole thing."

"Great!" I spin around in the chair and stop with my legs straddled on either side of his. "So, now I get to see the rest of it?" Both eyebrows bounce for a second.

"Uh, well…sure. What I can show you, anyway." He takes a step back, clearing the way, and I take the opportunity and stand beside him. "Though, there are a few things that I want to cover first."

It's deep breath time—for both of us.

"All right, well, let's start with one of the early questions." He pauses, and I can't judge why. "I work here as a behavioral psychologist. Specifically, I study the behavior of zombies," he glances around, "as I'm sure you could guess."

Oh, you've got to be…. "Are you telling me that, since the day we met, you've been secretly analyzing me? Figuring me out in your own way?"

"No!" His face scrunches up in complete shock. I don't buy it for a second. "No. Well, maybe. A little." He finally nods. "Yes, I have. Sorry." Now the poor boy looks positively wounded. "I can't help it. I've tried not to be blatant about it."

"You…haven't. I…. Yeah, I'm sure you can't help it." Quick breath. "So, what did you figure out?"

"About you?"

"Yeah, smart boy! Tell me all about me!"

"Oh no. No way. Let's just say that everything I've seen from you has been positive enough to keep me right at your side."

Without hesitation, he claps his hands and I jump just slightly. "So! Let's move on to the rest of the facility!"

"Wasn't there more you wanted to tell me first?" Oh come on! I wasn't teasing that much.

"Well, the second part is more me admitting to a lie—or really a half lie." He is actually biting his bottom lip, and I'm more than a little nervous myself, actually. "I have dealt with zombies in person before."

Whew. In grand scheme of things that's not too bad. "Well, okay, that's...okay."

"It's only a half lie! I really haven't ever been up close with a zombie outside before. I've only ever encountered them...in here."

Those words rattle around in my head for a couple of seconds. "In here? There are zombies in here?"

"Yeah. Lots, actually." He winces a little.

Thinking about it, that makes perfect sense. "For study purposes. If you're going to study zombies, you need zombies to study."

"Exactly!" Both hands go up, so I either gave him the response he was hoping for or I just scored a touchdown. "You would be surprised how many people freak out when they find out about the test subjects."

"Test subjects? Wow, that sounds so clinical, but then this would be the right place for that kind of term, wouldn't it?"

"Yes, it is, but it's not a big deal. You'll pick them up quickly." His smile turns much softer. "And now we move on to the physical portion of our tour."

He takes a couple of steps, glancing at me to make sure I'm following, and then paces straight over to the door on the back wall.

I'm not sure what I was expecting. I suppose I should have seen this one coming, given the way that everything else looks around here.

Like the rest of the facility, this area is a series of glass walls, one after another, lining the perimeter of the room. Separate chambers all divided by clear walls, carefully indicated by a pair of blue lines about six inches wide that run around each of the walls. I suppose that's so people don't wander around bumping into them constantly.

The contents of those rooms is very visible. Zombies. Lots and lots of zombies. Each room—and I'm guessing there are probably twenty of them at least—has at least a handful of zombies in them. At a glance they all have the same appearance of the ones I would see at The Mouth. They are simply stepping around the room aimlessly, drifting from one place to the next with no obvious cause or purpose. The only big difference is that they don't have very far to walk.

Groups of people—teams of researchers, I suppose—are doing their own milling about, bringing carts loaded with food to some of the rooms, or standing with charts in hand, or simply walking to and from stations or talking to other workers.

"Welcome to the testing grounds." Terry almost sounds excited. Thinking on it, I suppose he is—I know I am.

Though I do have to give him the eye. "Testing grounds? Is it somebody's job to come up with odd names for everything around here?"

"Clever names. Not odd." He laughs. Good. Don't want to wander into offending him by accident. Though, thinking on it,

I did just work at a place with something called The Mouth, so maybe I shouldn't pick on him about this.

"Okay, so, what are we testing?"

"Pretty obvious." He points over to a team loading what appears to be chunks of beef into a large drawer that would move things from one side of the wall to the other.

"They're feeding them?"

"That's right. That team is feeding that particular study group, while that team there," he points to a different gathering of people carrying what appear to be computer tablets, "is registering the results."

"And what are the results?" Wow. That sounds like a stupid question now that I've asked it.

"That's what we're here to find out." Which is exactly the answer I already knew.

"Okay, well, give me the tour, then." This time I gesture out, urging him on.

He takes a few steps and I follow. "Each of these rooms is set up to give us some insight into the means that a zombie takes when its eating. Its approach and procedure when finding its next meal."

"So, a small version of what we did at the F.O.O.D.Z. facility?" We didn't have someone with a computer tablet, though.

"Sort of. You were more working as distribution, though. What we're doing is trying to figure out the core behind them. The cause rather than the effect."

Well, thanks for making my last job seem so important. "Ah, I see."

"Okay, let me show you the groups." He moved towards the room where the beef cart had just been.

"Groups? The scientists?"

"No, I mean the groups. The different collections of zombies that we are studying. For example," he stops in front of the room containing the zombies currently chewing on chunks of cow, "this is the meat group. Here we have beef," he pointed towards the next—oh hell, let's go ahead and call them what they are, cells, "there's pork, and then chicken, and another chicken, and—well, there are currently five chickens, and then we get to one seafood."

"Why so much chicken?"

He shrugs at me. "Actually, we have more beef than we have chicken, but chicken is easily the second most popular. Though the beef factions tend to be a little more picky about what type of beef they want."

"Huh, well, okay." I do a slow turn, taking in the various cells and their current inhabitants. "So, what are the other groups?"

"Putting it in simplest terms, we have meat, fruits and vegetables, dairy, and—because we didn't really want to classify it with the others—the fast food group." His hand gestures with each class, giving me a rough idea where each of these groups sit.

"Fast food, eh?" The corner of my mouth curls up into a not-at-all-mocking smirk.

"They're pretty fanatical about it, actually." He nods with confidence to support his claim.

"I can imagine. Fast food can do that to anyone—living or dead. Are they the most dedicated group you've got?"

"No, actually." He takes a few steps and I follow him, until we stop in view of another cell filled with a dozen or so zombies who are standing perfectly still. "This is the one that never seems to change."

"What do they eat?" They look normal to me.

"Apples. No matter what we try to feed them, they always want apples. Every other group in here has changed their diet at one point or another, but the only thing these zombies want are apples. Day in, day out."

"Seems rather limiting." Poor things.

"Hey, I can't control what zombies want. All I can do is try to figure out why."

"I thought you said that you were able to change what the others wanted?"

"Not exactly." He ponders a moment. "It's more a case of hit or miss. One group will stop eating and then we bring the new food, trying a variety of options until we figure out what they want. If we're lucky they start muttering something about it. It's really not that dissimilar to what you would do out in a feeding facility."

"Okay, so how are you able to keep them all grouped up like this, then? If they change what they eat, shouldn't they move from meat to fruit to dairy to…whatever?"

"Yeah, they should." He looks around. "I keep trying to figure that out myself, but, for whatever reason, once they start down a group, they tend to stay in that group. Meat moves to new meat. Vegetable to new vegatable. And on and on." He laughs. "It's why we're doing the research. To figure stuff like that out."

Once more I look around and see some cells that weren't part of what he already showed me. "What about those sections?"

I hear a sharp intake of breath through teeth and discover Terry standing there with a rather concerned expression. "Those are...special cases."

"Special cases?" Oh no. The poor guy. I see what's going on. "Hey, Terry, don't worry about this. I'm not going to judge you. This is your job and it won't change the way I think of you."

"I hope you mean that," he replies, hiding as much concern as he can.

"Trust me." I try to give him the same type of smile that he has given me so many times already.

"Okay." Another deep breath gives him a moment to pause. "Okay, well, those are two special case groups. One of them we aren't feeding at all. We're wanting to see what happens when zombies are denied food for an extended period of time."

Part of me is terrified to know the answer to this but I still ask, "What does happen?"

"The initial reaction is urgency and demand, trying to find whatever food they are eating with some anxiousness, but that quickly degrades to violence. They'll beat on the walls and the glass, just lashing out with no apparent pattern. Eventually, though, they become rather passive. They just stand there, waiting."

"Waiting for what?" My voice is barely above a whisper.

"We wondered that, too—until we opened the door. It only took a second for them to react, and they rushed the door, almost killing the staff member as they pushed their way out into the main chamber." He shakes his head. "Apparently they were waiting for a chance to escape."

"Or to eat," I mumble. "They were starving and desperate."

"They aren't alive, Cici. They can't starve."

"Has anyone told them that?" I hope that didn't come out as snarky as it sounded to me. Change subjects, quick. "What about the other group? You said there were two."

"The last group is where we…" He pauses and looks away from me. "The last group is given live animals, so that we can see what they'll do with them."

I must have heard that wrong. "What?"

Slowly, he turns back to me. "We put live animals in the rooms with those zombies to see how they'll react. To find out if they'll go so far as to kill for food."

The taste of bile finds its way up to the back of my throat. "And?"

"And…sometimes. It's not consistent by any means. Some animals will be perfectly fine, and other times they don't last five minutes." He shakes his head, and I can almost see the images he's trying to get rid of as he does.

"That's…that's horrible." My eyes close tight.

"It's necessary," he replies. "It's not as though any of us take pleasure in seeing it happen, but until we can figure out why the zombies do any of the things they do, then we aren't safe. As long as they exist, we can never be truly safe."

"I try not to fall into that type of thinking." It's a good lie. I hope he buys it.

"I'm sure." His hand falls onto my back and I let in linger there for a moment before turning towards him.

His eyes border between concern and pity, and there is no way that I'm going to let either of those things take over right now. I spot another set of doors on the far wall and push on through to the next part of the conversation.

"So, what about those doors?" I ask with a nod towards them.

"Oh, those are not for you. Past your pay grade, so to speak, and you aren't allowed to go back there." He steps between me and the doors, gently turning me back the other way, despite the fact that we're easily twenty feet away from them.

"Do you get to go back there?" If I can't go, I can at least ask.

"I…do. I don't go very often, as it doesn't really relate to my specific area of study, but I have been back there a few times for various reasons."

"Such as…?" Come on. You know you want to tell me.

"Can't say. Sorry." His smile tries to have its regular charm, but either he's off a step or I'm just not in the mood to be charmed right now.

"Uh huh."

"Well, that's the basics. Let's get you back out to your desk and start going over your initial responsibilities here." He stops and looks at me more directly. "I'm thrilled that you're here, Cici."

"Thanks," I say with sincerity. He can be so nice sometimes. Then, as I look past him at the latest in a string of forbidden doors, I also remember that he's very big on keeping secrets— and far too good at it. "I'm sure it's going to be an interesting job at the very least."

Chapter Sixteen

"So, tell me a little about yourself."

Oh God, not that question. Ask me to juggle three glass jars filled with scorpions before asking me that damned question.

"Not really much to say. Just your run-of-the-mill woman who just happens to be adjusting to a new job." I hope that's enough. It isn't, of course, I realize that, but I still leave room for hope.

"Thank you." Ms. Dunn wasn't directing that gratitude my way, but towards the waiter who just dropped off another plate of sushi. She sure can put away a lot of the stuff, too. Never been a big fan myself, but I don't hate it, and I'd rather she be happy with at least where we're having lunch. Every little advantage on making a good impression, after all. "And how is the adjustment going?" Now we're back to me.

"Well, I'm on day two, really, so…good I guess? Nothing bad has happened, and I've only felt like an idiot two or three times, so I can't really complain." And there I go showing my amazing awkwardness in these situations once more.

"Give it time, you'll adjust." Her hand moves with a bit of unexpected grace as she maneuvers her chopsticks. There is an art to them I think, at least far more than people credit. It's like anything, though. You can know how to do something or use a tool, but making it into something worth looking at, well, that's a gift.

"To be honest, at the moment I'm still really trying to grasp what it is I'm supposed to be doing here at all." I raise a finger, still a little too intimidated to raise a whole hand. "I know, I know. You told me that I give a new perspective. That my personal experience in the field will help out somehow. Terry says the same thing. I guess I'm still trying to figure out exactly how."

"Don't worry, you will." A piece of food travels from plate to mouth, making a momentary stop in a soy and wasabi mix on the way. One thing that I state in favor of sushi is that it makes for an attractive meal.

"I suppose so," I don't think my words come out as more than a mumble.

"So, tell me about you and Terry."

Say what? "What about me and Terry?"

She chuckles and a lightness falls across the table. "That's what I'm asking. How long have you two been dating? How did you meet? You know, the works."

"Well, um, we haven't been dating that long, a little more than a month, and—as cliche as this sounds—we met at a bar." Odd when this type of question comes up and you suddenly realize that you haven't given it any thought. "I guess it was just luck. He was at the bar and he bought me a drink. I thought he was cute and things just grew from there."

She chews and swallows down some of her lunch. "Serious? Or are you just in it for fun? At least at this point?"

"I...well, I guess it's getting serious. I mean, I just moved in with him—at least on a temporary basis. It's funny, I've always said—well, since the whole zombie thing, anyway—that I wouldn't be in any serious relationship." I pause for a sigh. "Seems like that's not gonna hold up."

"It will if you want it to." Both chopsticks point at me like twin claws from an insect. "You are in control of your life. If you want to have a serious relationship, do it. If you don't, then don't. There is nothing that says you have to do anything in your life."

"Yeah, right." My fork pushes around the food on my plate. Some kind of grilled beef, but not teriyaki. I can't remember what it's called.

"Cici," my eyes pull up to hers, "it is your life, no one else's."

"I...." My head tilts to the right. "Forgive me if I'm being rude, but did you just call me Cici?"

"I did." She has a surprisingly light smile.

Now I get to decide what to say to my new boss, and just how bad that's going to hurt me in the future. Yay, me. "I thought you didn't like using first names. Something about becoming too familiar at work."

"We're not at work." Nimble slivers of bamboo pluck another bite from the plate. "So, while we're here, call me Deborah."

Strange rules, but I'm not going to argue with her. The laugh that sneaks out, however, might still get me in trouble. "Okay, Deborah."

"What?" she asks. "Ah! Let me guess, the name 'Bo' popped into your head."

"Uh, yeah, actually." I wince.

"No worries, it's not like I hadn't heard it before."

Slowly my head gives a nod. "And how do you feel about it? How did you get it?"

"Deborah. Bo is right there in the middle." She takes a quick sip of water. "I think it was my second week on the job that the first man used that nickname—and yes, it's almost always men who use it—because I busted his balls about the crappy work he was doing. With my size and demeanor," she shrugs, "I guess it was inevitable. And to answer your other question, no it doesn't bother me. It did for a while, but now I like to have that mystique around me."

Another laugh snorts out of me, accompanied by a shake of my head. "I'm not sure I could handle that. I don't like being disrespected."

"Well, I suppose I don't see it as disrespect. It's more of a coping mechanism for the men at work. In an odd way it's flattering."

We stare at each other for a full second. "That's a really messed up attitude."

"What's messed up about it?" she asks with a chuckle.

"The cavalier way you approach it." My hands go up reflexively. "I couldn't do that."

"But being called Cici doesn't bother you?" She's tapping her chopsticks on the plate lightly. I'm hoping that's because she's trying to line them up with each other.

"No. I've been called Cici since I was a little kid."

She picks up another bite of sushi. "Well, I just got my nickname a little later in life." She pops it in her mouth and makes quick work of it. "Now, if they were calling me something else—something that wasn't actually a name or nickname, then I'd be pissed."

"Okay, okay, fine," I lean in slightly, "but they are using a man's nickname because they can't handle you being female. You have to admit there is something messed up with that."

"I'm sure Bo Derek will be happy to hear that she's a man." She stares down at the table, and I can see the smug in her eyes.

"You know what I mean," I almost growl.

"I do, but again," she looks back up at me, "it doesn't bother me. I do come across somewhat masculine, I realize, so as long as they keep it on this level, I'm good. If anyone—male or female—crosses the line, then they are out. Plain and simple."

My mouth purses up and I suck a bit of air through my teeth. She raises an eyebrow.

"What did you do?" I wish her tone was a little less serious.

"I, uh, I…came up with a new nickname for you." Why the hell did I tell her that?

"Really" Both eyebrows are now up. "What is it?"

"Didi." I pause, waiting for some kind of reply, and then add, "At least it's a girl's nickname."

Her head slowly begins to nod up and down, and then, thankfully, a smile starts to creep onto her face. "That was what my aunt used to call me."

"Really?" Yay! I'm not going to be fired—or worse.

"Sure did. I was never a big fan of it, but I loved my aunt, so I never told her to stop." The tips of her chopsticks swirl around in the wasabi and soy mixture beside her plate. "And don't worry, calling me that is hardly an insult." The light laugh that comes from her is the best sound I've heard all day. "Don't call me Debbie, though. I hate that."

My relief must have been obvious from the expression on her face.

"So, changing subjects slightly," she says calmly, "what is it you want for yourself, Cici?"

Didn't I already go through the interview process? Or is this the interview? Am I doing the five-years-from-now thing? "I'm not sure what you mean? Is this about Terry again?"

"No. No, this is about you. I'm just curious what it is that you want. What are your goals, dreams, hopes…that kind of thing."

"I don't know." I've heard these words in my head a hundred times at least. "I'd like to say that I have something that I want to accomplish or some…thing…that I want to see done in my life, but since the zombies I just…." I shrug. "What's the point?"

Bringing the two chopsticks together, she carefully places them on a rest off to the side. "The point is that you are alive. Just because every day we find ourselves surrounded by death, there is no reason to stop living. Don't let the outside become your inside." She leans towards me slightly. "The only way that we can possibly overcome what has happened is if we don't give in. We have to stay alive."

Okay, I blink a couple of times. "I wasn't expecting that kind of speech."

"It's not a speech," she picks up her chopsticks and gets back to eating, "it's the truth."

"Well, then it's the truth disguised as a speech," I counter.

"I don't give speeches." Now she's being obstinate.

"Well, let me turn it around on you, then," let's see how she handles this, "what do you want? What are your goals?"

She stares at me for a long moment, slowly chewing the bite in her mouth. I watch as the pleasant woman who I've been sharing a meal with slowly melts away, replaced by the more strict and demanding boss who I dealt with yesterday.

"Isn't it obvious?" she asks.

I feel rather stupid for not having an answer for her.

"I want the zombies gone. I want the world returned to normal—or what we remember normal once being. I want to wake up and turn on the television and see a weather report and not a warning system for the latest outbreak. More than anything, I want to be completely out of a job, because the only place that a zombie will ever appear is in a history book or a story."

Damn. Why can't I talk like her?

"Yeah, I like the sound of that, too."

"Well, you have a chance to make it happen," she says as plain as day. "You're part of a team that is working towards that exact goal."

I take a deep breath. "I don't know what I'll be able to do, but I will certainly do it."

"That's all we can ask."

She smiles and I smile back at her. For that moment—that one exact moment—everything felt right in the world once again, and I wanted nothing more than to keep it going forever.

Chapter Seventeen

It's been a week, and so far, so good. I've gotten into a pretty good rhythm here, or at least more of one than I expected by this point. Right now my initial duties include feeding several of the different cages of zombies, and then recording their reactions. How quickly they eat. How much they eat. Y'know, that kind of thing.

Today, however, my routine is being thrown off a bit. It seems that I am going to be attending my first real meeting, of sorts. The two scientists I met on my first day here—Roger and Demarius—have asked me to sit in with them again, I assume to go over the same things that we already covered, only this time with the ability to tell me more of what is going on.

"Thanks for coming, Ms. Cole," Roger says with a large grin on his face. He has that very distinct expression of a kid in the depths of a candy store.

"It's not a problem, and call me Cici. Ms. Cole just sounds like you want to sell me something." A quick nod goes over to Demarius, who, thankfully, chuckles at my lame joke. "So, what am I here for? What's going on?"

"First, let me say thank you, too," Demarius chimes in. "As to what you are here for, well, it's basically the same thing that we talked about a few days back, but we've gotten clearance to take it up to the next level." He steps back and motions to one of the chairs around the table.

Much like in the first room where we met, the tables in this room sit high, with appropriate seating around them. There are six chairs around the table right now, but there could easily be another six squeezed in if the need was desperate. Unlike the other tables, these have a rather nice feature: a monitor built into the tabletop. If I were to guess—and I'm not that great at estimating this kind of thing—I would say that it was the equivalent of about a forty-inch television. Lying flat like it is the dimensions seem huge, though.

There is an unusual degree of privacy to this room, too. The walls—just as glass as any other—have a film on the outside of them, making it difficult to see any details inside. Even more so than the frosted glass. Seeing out, however, isn't a problem at all, and I glance up to see some of my co-workers wandering about on their regular business for the day. I scan around looking for Terry, but it seems he is off somewhere else.

It's odd. Two of the glass walls look into the rooms that I've already been through. The other two seem to be looking into a hallway. A normal sized one, and not the monster that Ms. Dunn escorted me through on my first day. A couple of people walk past that I've never seen before and I almost pay attention to what they look like, but Roger's motion moves my eyes back to the moment at hand.

The two of them sit down side-by-side, and I take a chair across from them. Light flares up from below as the monitor screen casts an odd bluish tint over the room.

"We'd like to go over a theory that we've been working on," Roger states. "And I want to stress that it is just that: a theory."

"One that we are feeling better and better about as each day goes past," Demarius follows up. His hand moves, revealing a small black item that looks vaguely like a remote control for the television, only with fewer buttons and a wheel-like device in the middle of it. As his fingers dance across it the image on the screen changes quickly. I see several folders open and close, and screens scroll by as though there were on the world's fastest slideshow. Finally, they come to a rest, just as Demarius' hand loosens his grip on the remote.

My mind reels as the image comes clearly into focus on the screen.

"That's Curly," I mutter aloud.

"Excellent!" Roger shouts. "That was the first thing that we wanted to confirm. That this is, indeed, the zombie you called Curly."

It's just a still of him in the field outside The Mouth at my old job, except I have no idea where they were standing to take that photo. I wrap my brain around the options, trying to picture anything that might be at the place where someone with a camera had to be standing, but I keep coming up empty.

"How did you get that?" I ask.

"We've had the facility under surveillance since we had our first conversation with you," Roger explains. "We've been looking for a specimen like him since we first formed our theory, and everything that you told us led us to believe that he was perfect."

"You're sure it's him?" Demarius asks. "Absolutely sure."

My head bobs up and down. "Yeah, that's him. Why are you watching him?"

"We would love to explain." Roger shifts in his seat, pulling himself up and straightening his shirt. "You see, for a couple of years now, Demarius and I have been pursuing the concept that not all zombies are the same. That there are distinct levels—"

"Classes," Demarius interrupts.

"Yes, classes, of zombies that co-exist together. We aren't sure exactly how many there might be, but we believe there are at least three." Roger nods to Demarius, who immediately goes back to his remote.

"The vast majority of zombies—the ones that you see every day—are what we are calling the Betas. They are the ones that move about mindlessly in large packs and generally create the majority of the threats that we have to deal with, in that they have the larger numbers so what they do has the biggest impact on human society." Roger seems a little too excited about this.

"Okay," I answer slowly, "so what are the other two?"

Vaguely humanoid shapes, twisted with decay, flitter past on the screen. He finally comes to a stop on a shadowy figure, somewhat blurred and hidden behind a few shrubs, walking away from the camera, glancing back over his shoulder.

"We are calling them Alphas and Omegas." As Demarius says that, I almost can hear dramatic music swell in the background. "The Omegas are the rare type of zombie that has become solitary. One that moves around with almost no connection to the rest of their society. They live below our normal radar, mostly because that's the way they want it to be. They avoid humans, and indeed, other zombies."

"Wow. That's…." I lean in a bit. "Have you guys seen a zombie like that? I've never seen one that acted like that before."

"Well, no," Demarius answers weakly. "That's what makes them theoretical. It makes sense, though, that there are zombies that we never encounter."

"And we aren't saying that it is limited to just the Omegas," Roger clarifies. "We may have to modify our ideas to fit in with two, three, or maybe far more types of zombies that we don't encounter. It's possible that we've only touched the tip of the zombie iceberg, so to speak."

A part of my brain sees the logic in this perfectly. Why wouldn't there be multiple types of zombies? Ones that do different things and have different lifestyles? There is another huge part of my brain that is screaming that these are monsters that have been formed from lifeless corpses, so…what the hell?

"The Alpha's are almost the opposite," Demarius brings my mind back to the matter.

"Yes, we believe that Alphas spend the vast majority of their time interacting with the Betas, and, for lack of a better word, are their leaders," Roger explains—with a completely serious expression, I might add. The image on the screen changes, once more ending up with a different—though still oddly positioned—picture of Curly.

It doesn't take a huge amount of insight to see where this is going. "You think that Curly is an Alpha."

Both of their faces light up as they glance at each other, then back at me.

"Exactly!" Roger exclaims with glee. I swear I've seen kids at amusement parks that weren't as happy as these two right now. "He is our first real link in this new chain. We're hoping that studying him will allow us to identify his kind. If we can do that, then potentially we'll be able to guide them along and create, rather than react."

"Which is why you were so interested in how I was able to get him to eat the cereal. Okay, this is making sense." There is actual potential here. These two might truly be able to help the whole world if they are right.

"Yes! And now...." Roger trails off.

I stare at him, expecting more. The continuation of his thought finally comes from Demarius.

"Now we need you to serve as our eyes. To date, you are the only person who has spotted an Alpha in any way. Whatever it was you saw in him, we are hoping you will see in others."

My eyes dart back and forth between them. "I saw him showing off a cabbage. Anyone can spot that type of thing."

"Ah!" One of Roger's fingers darts up, seemingly pointing towards the ceiling with authority. "According to Terry, though, you had already named Curly before you saw him showing off his cabbage. You reacted to his display only after becoming familiar with him."

"Well, what girl wouldn't react to a man showing off his cabbage." I didn't want to say that, but I did it anyway. "Still, it's not that big a deal. I'm not special."

"What if you are?" Demarius says softly.

It's a good thing that I practiced staring in confusion as a child, otherwise my reaction would have seemed very amateur. "I beg your pardon?"

"That's, uh...." Roger looks to Demarius and gives him a quick nod. The images on the screen flicker past once again. "That's the last part of what we wanted to talk to you about." The images slow, becoming a gradual slideshow of pictures, pausing one after the other, each one showing zombies and humans in the same shot.

"We've been accumulating data about human-zombie relations for years now, trying to find a pattern. Something that we could use to predict what the zombies were going to do next and how we could prepare for it," Roger begins.

"Sadly, there isn't any," Demarius picks right up. "At least, there isn't any sort of behavior that we were looking for." He points to the current picture on the screen. Five people—three men and two women—stand near a group of at least a dozen zombies, but it's hard to tell. "Sometimes zombies are very passive, not reacting to the humans around them at all. Other times however," a new image pops up on the screen, displaying what seems to be seven—no, eight—humans holding up a barricade to keep out only three zombies, "you get aggression."

"Could just be a numbers thing," I answer. "Maybe they just feel more comfortable if they have greater numbers."

They look at each other and smile. "Think about what you just said? They feel better in greater numbers?" Roger says.

"I said more comfortable." It's a small point, but this is for science, right?

"That's not the important word. You said 'feel,'" he clarifies. "Zombies aren't alive. They don't feel."

"At least not the way we think of it," Demarius adds. "We know for a fact that zombies will defend themselves if attacked, indicating a survival instinct of some sort. We both believe that it goes further. That the zombies are able to react to their surroundings in any number of ways. Their surroundings and other stimulus, as well."

"Which includes certain people," Roger jumps back in. "It is very possible that the only reason you were able to spot this Alpha behaving normally is because they felt comfortable around you. More so than they do other living humans."

What the…? "What are you guys saying? That I'm some kind of…zombie whisperer?"

"Not the term that I would have used," Roger half whines, "but, essentially, yes."

"You have got to be kidding me!" Seriously, they have to be kidding, right? This is a prank they play on new employees. Terry is going to burst in laughing any second.

Any second now.

"We're completely serious." Dammit, Demarius, you were supposed to start laughing when Terry burst in!

"And just what the hell is that supposed to mean? What is it you want from me?" One of my feet turns out from the chair, trying to make its escape ahead of me.

"Nothing dangerous, I assure you!" Roger holds up both hands. "We just want to observe you dealing with some of the zombies we have here. Without others around. Just you."

My eyes narrow. "I'm not sure we have the same definition of dangerous."

"We'll be monitoring you," Demarius says. "Cameras everywhere and security ready to burst in whenever anything starts to go bad."

"Starts to go bad?"

"Before then!" Roger clarifies, in his most emphatic tone. "The important thing is that we are not going to put you in any immediate danger. Every precaution will be taken. And think of what we might learn. What we're doing here isn't safe, but it is amazingly needed."

Dammit. I let out a long sigh. "How many zombies are we talking about here?"

"At one time or overall?" Demarius asks.

"You have to clarify that?" I snap back. It is entirely possible that I'm still being a tad defensive here.

"No more than six at a time," Roger says.

"And overall?" I ask.

"Uh, well…all of them." He smiles. It is the most awkward and desperate smile I've ever seen in my life. His lips are crooked and his teeth are a little too carefully clenched and lined up together. A look over at Demarius reveals a face that isn't smiling, but there is every ounce of desperation in his eyes as there is in his partner's.

"It's why we're here, Cici," Roger adds as his face softens.

This is unbelievable. Not the zombie theory, that I can follow with no problem, as far fetched as it might be. Not even that they are wanting me to deal with zombies one-on-one. I've done that before, after all, I'm just not going to tell them that. No, the unbelievable part is what comes next.

"When do we start?" I ask.

Chapter Eighteen

I'm staring at a zombie. Oh sure, I've been doing that for years now, both privately and professionally, but this time is different. This time I'm locked in a small room with four of them, and I'm all by myself.

This might not have been my finest career move.

"Hello." Start simple. Break the ice. Move on from there.

Of course it would help if the zombie reacted in any way at all. Right now all four of them are simply shambling around the room, occasionally turning around and shambling back the other way when they come to one of the glass walls.

There is one female and three male zombies here, and I step in front of the smallest male, waving my hand gently. "Hey there!" Sure, be forceful with your greeting. That should do it.

He walks up to me, opens his mouth and releases the ungodly odor that is apparently living inside of him. Thankfully, the venting system quickly pulls the scent up and out of the room, but I still get a nose full of it first. I wave my hand in front of my face again, but this is to move the air and not to say hello. He follows my hand movement for a moment and doesn't turn away from me.

Maybe I should try a different tactic.

Standing up as straight as I can, I smile. My lips are pulled back so far that my face is actually hurting from the effort. The zombie stares at me, and thankfully he's doing it with two eyes. I look into his dark, cloudy eyes, trying to find something, anything, there for me to connect with and discover. Any spark that will show me that there is an intelligence behind his actions.

And then he turns to the side and shambles off towards another wall.

With a shake of my head I turn towards the camera and shrug my shoulders. Demetrius and Roger are on the other side, watching my every move. I even get the feeling that Terry might be there, too, since this is my first real run through this program.

For the past two weeks we've been setting up this testing zone. It's located right next to the main room where the test subjects are contained, allowing for easier transport to this special container. Resting in the center of this new room, the containment chamber has four glass walls and a glass ceiling. In fact, the only thing that isn't glass in this thing is the floor, which is—I assume from the feel of it—reinforced concrete.

The lighting in the room is kept at a low level, basically the equivalent of twilight—at least currently. The lights in here can be raised up to shine like mid-day, or they can be lowered to simulate dim moonlight. For the first try, we thought that going with a neutral level would be the best option.

And even though I turned to look at that specific camera, there are a total of twelve cameras currently focused on this space and what's going on inside it. Which, at the moment, isn't much of anything.

"Keep going, Cici. You've got this." I hear Roger's voice come through clear as day through the communication bud I'm wearing.

"Yeah, right," I mumble. I'm sure that he hears me through the mic, though.

"Relax." Terry's voice confirms my theory about his location. "No one said this was going to be easy."

"Or possible," I answer—and instantly regret. "Ignore that. Let me try again."

Okay, so talking didn't work. Smiling didn't work. I guess.... I stand before the same zombie, carefully interjecting myself between him and the next wall available. For a moment I worry about him stopping, fearing that he might have decided that the shortish-haired blond thing in front of him is an annoyance—or worse.

Thankfully, he stops, his face slowly moving around to stare at me with the same complete lack of...anything, really, that he had before. The important part is that I have his attention. I think.

Raising my hand, I place it, palm out, between our faces. I leave just enough gap to see his eyes moving to look at the hand, and just to be certain I move it slightly to watch his eyes track it, which he does.

"Okay, let's see how this goes," I mutter aloud, mostly just to remind myself the odds of what I'm doing having any result. Then, with all the style and panache that the action deserves, I take my hand and begin slowly patting myself on the head.

His eyes are still locked on my hand, watching as it rhythmically moves up and down, a soft thudding slap echoing slightly in the room as palm meets hair. His head seems to almost bounce along with my hand, watching the constant pattern repeat. Out of the corner of my eye I can see his hand move, rising up in front of him gradually. It moves past his midsection to shoulder level, and my heart skips a beat.

Until he turns around and staggers off towards the opposite wall.

"Dammit!" I shout as I throw my hand down to my side.

"It's okay, Cici," Roger's voice calmly says in my ear. "We weren't looking for a home run in our first at bat."

"Good, because I suck at baseball," I grumble.

The chuckle that comes back through my earpiece puts me slightly at ease. "I'm going to step out. Collect myself for a bit," I announce.

"No problem." There is a soft click in the transmission, and I assume that he has turned off the mic on his side.

The entrance—or from this side, exit—to this container uses the kind of lock you see in super-spy movies. Basically, I put my hand up to what looks like yet another glass plate, a light moves through it scanning my palm print, and the door unlocks. I put mine up, I hear a click, and then I open the door and move into the ante-chamber. Yes, the room has an ante-chamber, just in case a zombie tries to rush through with me, which thankfully doesn't happen. One more repeat of the first mechanism on the next door and I'm free and clear of the space.

"You okay?" Terry's voice in my ear causes me to jump. I guess the mic wasn't off after all.

"Frustrated. Flustered. Something else that starts with the letter F." I move over to the table in the room, not bothering with a chair and instead choosing just to lean against it.

"I'll be right there," he says softly.

I surprise myself with the response. "No. No, don't. I'm just… I'm going to go offline for a few. Clear my head. I'll be right back."

Before I can hear a reply my hand flashes past my ear, taking the transceiver with it. As I step away I drop it on the table and head for the door without a glance backwards.

Questions start to overwhelm me. I have no idea what made me think that I was going to be able to do what they want. I'm nothing special. I never have been. All my life I've just been barely good enough, and always trying to be better. My mother and father always wanted more from me. They told me that it was because they thought I was capable of anything and they wanted to see me become something special. Yeah. Well, if you read that sideways it's easy to see it another way: I was always a disappointment whom they felt never did live up to her potential.

Oh, I'm sure they would never have said those words, but then again, they didn't have to—I already heard them. Maybe that's the reason I ran away. It isn't the thought of seeing my dead parents potentially once more walking around the house, only with a serious hygiene issue among other things, but what they might think of me even now. What I might think of myself, even.

No. No, don't do this, Cici! You are here to do something special, and dammit you can. Just shake your head and clear the damn cobwebs out and…and….

And realize that you have no idea where you are. My head turns back and forth a few times and I spin in a circle. I did go out the door on the left, right? Or was I supposed to go out the door on the right and take a left?

Wow. I'm good.

Still, it's easy enough to retrace my steps. These back halls all pretty much look the same, and the walls here aren't even glass, so it's not too trying an issue to turn around and head from whence I came. Which would be a perfect plan if the doors were in the same pattern they were in the correct hallway.

Two fingers come up to the bridge of my nose, squeezing gently as I try to push back the frustration. The time it takes for my lungs to fill, hold, and exhale is enough to clear my head slightly. I know it's going to be one of the doors on my left, and that whole spatial awareness thing is giving me a clue to distance. Which makes this a bit of a guessing game, I suppose.

There is a hesitation as my hand hovers over the handle to the first door I'll try. It doesn't last, though, and I feel the cold metal turning in my grip. I push it in just enough to get a glance inside; two desks and a trio of filing cabinets stare back at me, devoid of any people. For a second I hesitate, wondering why anyone still uses a filing cabinet. I guess some things are good to have backed up with paper, but there isn't much, is there?

The question stays behind as I shut door number one and move on to the next selection in my private game show. Door number two is locked, which actually is a good sign. The lab door is sealed to anyone without proper clearance, which luckily, I have right now. With a wave of my id badge I try again, this time greeted by the familiar click of the metal giving permission to enter.

Once the door swings open, however, I immediately want to have that taken back. Something catches at the base of my throat, trying to push its way up and out of my body in a very unpleasant manner. I want to say that this is the worst smell that I've ever experienced, but the honest truth is that it's simply a smell that I haven't encountered this strongly in a while.

A single table sits in the middle of the room. On it is a single figure—I think. Its arms and legs are securely fastened to the four corners of the table, like some odd fetish contraption gone horribly wrong. The center of it is...everywhere. My mind tries to make sense of this, telling me a single large incision splits the center of the creature's body, splaying open the flesh widely. What would be the breastbone has been removed and it is sitting nearby in something that looks like an odd aquarium. One heart, a pair of lungs, and several other organs that I truthfully can't properly identify are lying beside the figure, resting on the table—but still attached to the inside of the poor creature, as though they were just sitting to the side while the middle was being cleaned or something.

Above its eyes a smooth incision creates a complete circle around the skull, penetrating both skin and bone. It takes an extra moment for me to fully realize that there are wires connected to long needles—probes, I suppose—inserted into the exposed brain. Dozens of wires snake down over the edge of the table and run in a tightly bound bundle towards the wall.

I think to myself that there should be blood, but there isn't. Why isn't there blood?

The answer is obvious of course, I just don't want to believe it. Or I suppose, I just don't want to acknowledge that, in spite of all the damage and mutilation, I still recognize him.

"Curly?" I whisper.

The nightmare before me is bad enough. I'm not sure that I'll ever be able to get that image out of my head. On the other hand, I'm quite positive that the following event will haunt me until my final day.

Small shudders seem to course over his flesh. At first the bile that has been welling up in my throat prepares itself for final release as I imagine something crawling up and through this dead man's flesh. It's only when I hear a gurgle rising from his throat that I realize the truth.

He's trying to turn to look at me.

I stagger back, the wall catching me before my body can move enough to fully reach the floor. In a blind desperation my hand plays along the wall, sliding up and down and to either side of me as I move along until finally finding the door handle. I hear it rattle as my hands do their best to operate the exit, but don't dare turn away from the zombie who is doing his best to move under the circumstances.

Memory kicks in and I spin around in a flash, popping my id card in front of the reader just long enough for the door to respond. With a resounding thud my knee strikes the edge of the door as I move past it. Tomorrow that will be a bruise that makes me wonder where I got it, but for now I'm out of that... whatever the hell that was.

Suddenly I am aware of my breathing. The air is rushing in and out of me so quickly that I'm on the verge of passing out. Taking another step away from the door I allow myself a moment to gather my thoughts. They aren't pleasant, but sadly, I don't have time to sort through them properly.

"…with the…overly confident…tomorrow morning…"

The words are broken apart by gaps of incoherence, but the ones I hear are clear enough. I know that voice. I will probably never forget that voice. A panic sets in, causing me to take a step back towards the door in front of me—which is quickly quelled by the image of Curly's body splayed apart on an examination table.

The voices are getting louder and I'm left with little options, but I choose the one that doesn't involve the latest in my long diet of nightmare fuel.

A few steps later I open the door to the office, seeing the filing cabinets lining the walls and the two desks sitting in the middle of it. With as much silence as I can muster, I step inside pulling the door almost closed, leaving just enough space for me to spy through the gap. I have to know. I have to see for myself.

She rounds the corner first. The same smartly tailored black outfit that she wore the night she came to my apartment fits her like a glove. Two other men are behind her, one of which I recognize. It's the man who spoke to me in the lobby the first day I was here. I don't recognize the other man, but judging from his clothing he seems to be a doctor of some sort. Behind them is the other one—the male counterpart to the woman— also dressed in the finely tailored black clothing.

They are speaking to each other, but I can't hear a word. Partially because of the door being mostly closed, and partially because the only sound that I can hear is the beating of my own heart. My eyes are functioning perfectly, however, and I watch as they turn and walk down the hall towards me.

And now is when my own stupidity comes crashing down around me. I can't shut the door. If I shut the door they'll hear it—or at least they could, and I won't take that chance. My only hope is that they will pass the door by, which, considering the security in this building, is hardly a likely scenario.

I'm trapped.

That doesn't mean that I'm giving up though, and with a small burst of energy I rush to the farther desk, pushing the chair at it out far enough for me to crawl underneath. It's not a hugely spacious desk, making it a tight fit, but I'm hardly in any situation to complain.

And then, I wait.

I'm sure it was less than a minute, but you never actually realize how long a minute truly is until you are desperately waiting for it to pass. The steady pounding of my blood through my veins is enough to keep me on edge, making it very difficult to suppress the growing desire to scream.

The slightest creak of the door brings that all to a sudden stop. My heart, my breathing, and all my desires are pushed down to almost nothing as I concentrate on the sounds that have invaded the room.

"See? I told you." It's the man's voice. The one from the lobby. I can almost hear him talking to me about the waterfall once more. "There is nothing here. It's just a door that wasn't fully closed."

"You will forgive me, sir, but it is my responsibility to make sure that is the case." She's speaking with that same light tone. Almost cheery. What the hell is wrong with her?

"And now that you have, can we move along?" he asks her.

"I haven't checked the room, sir." Her words stab me.

"Fine, here." The sound of footsteps move into the room, and I glance back, seeing a shadow loom beside the desk. The only thing separating us is a thin piece of metal acting as the back of a desk. "Now, I've searched the room, let's move along. Dr. Thomas says that we have a very limited window to observe his experiment, and I do not want to miss it."

"Sir—"

Her words are cut off by his quick response. "No. No, we're going. The two of you will be the death of me, I swear. I don't need you hovering over me every single minute of the day, you know."

"We're just doing our job, sir." From the tone of her reply, you would think that he just told her that she won a cheerleading contest.

"I know, dammit, but that doesn't mean I have to like it." His shadow disappears and his footsteps fade away towards the door.

"I appreciate your understanding, Dr. Zacek, sir. If you would just allow Alex and I to—"

The sound of her voice is cut off by a door clicking shut. I don't move for—well, I don't know how long I stay still, honestly. All I know is that I can feel my face flush and my finger freeze. Finally I move, climbing out of my hiding place and peeking around the edge, just to be sure that I am alone. Satisfied, I stand up and quickly tip-toe to the door, pressing my ear against it.

Nothing. No sound at all. I am left with the option of staying where I'm at, or taking a chance and opening this door and sprinting for escape. I choose the latter.

With every bit of delicate ease I can muster I crack open the door. The hallway beyond is empty and I waste no time in stepping through the opening and closing the door behind me with the same caution that I used to open it.

The way back to the part of the facility I know is to the left, and I rush that direction. As I pass by the door that holds Curly in his…condition…I hear the faint sound of voices, which only causes me to quicken my step.

The keypass on my hip fumbles through my fingers, but the faint click of the lock tells me that I moved it enough. I push through, relieved to see the huge glass cage holding the same zombies I left a short while ago. My heart soars to see Terry standing beside the table in the center of the room.

"Hey," he says in a calm, comforting tone. "Are you okay?"

"No!" I shout in a panicked, desperate voice. "We've got to get out of here. Right now. I've got to get out of here now!"

That got his attention. His whole body stiffens and he takes a step towards me. "What? What's wrong? What can I do?"

"They're here. I don't know how or why or…it doesn't matter. I've got to go." His arm fills my hand and I tug on it as I move past him, urging him towards the exit along with me.

"Who? What are you talking about?" Why is he not rushing along with me? It's like I'm having to drag him right now.

"Them! Those two people who came to my house! They're here. They're just down the hall. We have to go!" The exit isn't getting close fast enough, so I turn back to give him a direct order.

I just wasn't expecting the expression that I saw.

"Cici, I can explain…." He doesn't seem angry anymore. Nor does he look frightened. He looks odd.

"Explain what? Haven't you been listening? Those two…." Those two are in the building. Right next door, in fact, and Terry is standing in front of me right now.

I can feel the color leave my face.

"You knew that." The words come out barely a whisper. "You knew they were here." A tingle runs across my face. "They've always been here, haven't they? Oh my God. OhGodohGodohGodohGodohGod. You…they…."

There is a strong tremble that I feel as I put my fingers to my mouth. I'm not sure if it's my hands shaking or my lip quaking—or both.

"I can explain, Cici," he starts again.

"Explain?" The dam has broken. "What are you going to explain? That you knew about them coming to my place to terrorize me? That you didn't want to tell me about it because you would lose your job?" My hands are flying wildly around me. "Or is it that…." I freeze. "Oh God. You're the one who told them about me. You were…."

I don't wait for anything else. With a quick turn on the ball of my foot I race for the door. It opens and I don't stop. My feet move faster than I thought possible, and I'm amazed that I can see where I'm going through the tears that are streaming from my eyes.

There is no time to wipe them away. If I stop—if I slow down— there is a chance it will explode, that someone will step in front of me and I won't ever see the light of day again. The only sound that I allow myself to make is the ragged gasp of my breath as I sprint through the building.

Door after door opens in front of me, pushed aside by either my desperation or my momentum, and I frankly don't care which. When the warmth of the sunlight hits my face I discover that my fear reaches a new peak.

Across the parking lot is my car. I can see it from where I am, which gives me hope that I may actually make it. It's the thought that escape is that close that frightens me the most. The world can't be that cruel, can it?

My hand moves into my pocket, slowing me down slightly as I try to fish out my keys. The image from every horror movie I've ever seen plays over and over in my head. I make it to the car, the keys jangle in my hand and then drop to the ground, leaving just enough time for the pursuers to close the gap. Half of the time the protagonist gets away, and half of the time they are eaten by the monster.

When I reach the car I allow myself a second to look behind me. Nothing. There is no one that has even taken a step outside the building.

You know what? I don't care. The same desperate need pushes me on and I insert the key, turn the lock, open the door, and sit down inside. After a quick swallow, I put the key into the ignition and turn it, sparking the engine to life.

The scream of tires signals the next stage of my flight, and I don't bother slowing down until I reach my destination.

Chapter Nineteen

"I'm sorry for doing this to you, but I didn't know where else to go."

"Don't think twice about it!" Not only did Julie take me in the second I got to her place, but she called Mike right away to tell him what had happened. He swore that he was going to take care of it immediately.

That was almost two hours ago, and we still haven't heard back from him. I don't want to say that I'm worried and nervous about him not calling back, but...well, I just won't say it, then.

"Are you sure you don't want something to eat?" Julie asks me, reminding me again why she's going to make a great mother. "It wouldn't be a problem. I have some steaks in the freezer. I can thaw one out and cook it up for you in just a few minutes."

"I'm fine, thanks. I...I'm fine." I look down at the empty glass on the table in front of me. There is no way that I should be doing this, but that isn't going to stop me at all. "Any chance I can get another...." The ice cubes gently clink against the side of the glass as I shake it.

She sighs, and I can see the desire to give me a lecture hiding behind her eyes, but thankfully all she does is get up and take the glass from me. Immediately, I stand up and take it right back from her. "I know where everything is at. You don't need to make it for me, I just wanted to make sure it was okay that I steal more of your booze."

There is no argument, and Julie puts her left hand on the small of her back as she sits down. "I can't believe those two were there with you. And Terry! I just don't believe it."

I suppose we aren't really going to be able to talk about anything else for a bit, are we? "Not as shocked as I was, I bet." A couple of new ice cubes ring against the glass as I drop them in. The image of Curly on the slab flashes across my mind and I feel the glass slip from my hand and hit the counter just before I set it down. I don't say a word, letting it pass as glass slick from sweat. A couple of fingers of whiskey go into the glass, followed by a splash of tonic water. It's nice to have a friend who knows what you like to drink.

"So, what now?" Julie asks softly. "I mean, I assume you are never going back to that place, and I won't let you go to Terry's without Mike going with you so you can gather your things, but what then? Have you thought about where you're going to go or what you're going to do?"

Living in the south, and specifically Atlanta at the moment, my first instinct is to tell her that I'll worry about that tomorrow. It is another day, after all. "I haven't thought about it."

"Well, I want you to know that you can stay here as long as you want. You always have a room here with us," Julie tells me.

"I know." I sit back down across from her, smiling over the table. "Right now, you and Mike are the only consistent things in my life."

It's funny how you can call upon the gods of irony at any given time with any given statement. Take for example the fact that right after I said that, the front door opened and in stepped officer Mike Newmark in full uniform. He didn't look very happy.

"Mike!" Julie popped up from her chair as fast as her condition allowed and hurried over towards him. There was a quick hug between them and then Mike pulled back and looked over at me even as Julie continued to talk to him. "What did you find out? Did you go arrest those two people?"

He just walked past her and came over to the table. The expression on his face wasn't the happy one I was hoping to see when he got home.

"I spoke with my captain, Cici. Told them everything that you told me." He took a deep breath. "The only problem was that the CZC had already called to put in a complaint about you. They claim that there was a disturbance at the labs today, caused by you, leading to you being fired. And that, in response, you destroyed some property as you left and swore to make them pay. They claim you were irrational."

"What?" If there wasn't a table in front of me I would have popped straight up to a standing position. Instead, I just banged my thighs against it as I tried to stand anyway.

"I know, I know!" His hand goes up to try to calm me down. "I told my captain that there was no way there was any truth to that. You aren't that kind of person. So, he sent a detective crew over to check things out."

"Yeah?" Julie moves beside him looking up at his eyes. "And they found out the truth, right?"

"That entirely depends on what you think the truth might be." Oh boy. I don't like the sound of that. "Cici, I hate to ask this, but…" But you're going to ask it anyway, aren't you? "…are you telling us the truth?"

"Michael Johnson Newmark!" Woah, she used all three names. Julie is ticked. "How dare you suggest such a thing?"

"Mike, I'm telling the gospel truth. Why would I lie?" I explain immediately.

"I don't know, but I do know that they had video footage of you wrecking a lab and assaulting two staff members."

"What?" I'm sure my eyes are wider than my auditory surprise.

"Now, don't worry, they aren't pressing any charges."

I blink and clear away the shock in my eyes. "Well, that's good news." I push the chair back allowing me to finally stand up in indignation. "Are you serious? They…they had to fake that somehow! I never did anything like that!"

"Cici, look, I'm on your side. I'm just telling you that…." His hand moves to the back of his head. "I'm telling you that the police are on their side."

"They don't believe me. They think I'm making this up. You've got to be kidding me." For a moment I turn away, but quickly turn back to look him in the eye. "Do you believe me?"

"I…." He stares at me for a long second.

The sudden knock on the door causes all three of us to jump. I guess we're all feeling a little wired right now.

"Who's that?" I ask as Mike takes his first step towards the door.

He looks back at me over his shoulder. "I'm guessing it's someone who's trying to get us to come to the door."

Reaching his hand towards the door I have a sudden flashback and yell out in spite of myself. "Mike!" His hand jerks back and he turns to face me directly. Julie, only a step or two away from me, does the same thing. "Be careful."

He laughs. "I'm a cop, Cici. I've got this."

The door swings open easily as he answers it with a polite smile.

"Hi there! You must be officer Newmark."

Oh no.

"Yes. Can I help you?"

"Shut the door, Mike! Shut it now!" I scream as I scamper backwards.

"My name is Alice Alexandria, and I'm with the ZCTF." She's still talking. Why hasn't he shut the door? "May I come in?"

Mike hasn't moved, in fact. He's standing still, filling the doorway. "No," he says, and my heart races for a moment. "I'm sorry, miss, but I have company right now and I don't have time for any official work. If you'd like, you can stop by my precinct tomorrow. For some reason I think you might know where it is."

Damn. Go, Mike.

"Well, one of your guests is the reason I need to speak with you, actually. It would be much easier if you would just let me inside."

I've heard that before.

"I'm going to have to ask you to leave, miss." He's using that cop voice. The one that says don't-screw-with-me. Good.

"That isn't going to happen, Officer Newmark."

Everything moves in a sort of slow motion for a moment. I see Mike pushing on the door, attempting to close it—and the key word there is attempting. Before it can fully shut, a sharp crack, like a baseball bat hitting a home run, launches the door fully open once more, sending Mike staggering backwards.

The woman, Alice, calmly steps inside the house, shutting the door behind her.

In a single motion, I turn and grab Julie by the arm, making a move for the back door. Out of the corner of my eye I see Mike moving up towards her, and I vaguely hear him shouting something to her. Perhaps foolishly, I turn to look at them, watching as Mike pulls his pistol free from his holster. He doesn't even get a chance to properly aim it before Alice grabs it and twists, wrenching it free from his grip. I don't know exactly how she does it, but in less than a second the clip is ejected and the slide pops off the top of it, both of them falling harmlessly to the ground.

"Crap!" Julie is screaming, I think it's something about Mike but I'm not going to take the time to listen. It would be better if she weren't fighting me to make it out of the living room, though. And even better than that would be if I didn't see Alice's partner, Alex, walking in from the kitchen.

I freeze.

"No need to rush out, Miss Cole." He nods to what is happening behind me. "We'll have our conversation in just a moment."

Every part of me is dreading it, but I turn around and look anyway. There is no doubt that Mike knows what he is doing. Each time he moves in towards the woman it's clear that he has an exact plan of attack and the ferocity and motivation to make it happen.

I just wish it was working.

You would think that someone of Mike's size would have a clear advantage, even considering that Alice is larger than an average woman by a good handful of inches. I would say he still has four inches on her, after all.

He moves in with good speed, lowering his shoulder to take her down or drive her into the wall, maybe, but in a flash I see her hands move up behind his head and her knee move up to meet her hands. What's between them takes a harsh beating.

She doesn't relent. Holding on to his hair, she brings her knee up once, twice, and a third time. Then, before Mike even has the chance to fall down, her right elbow raises up and drives straight down into the back of his neck.

Mike falls to the ground like so much dirty laundry.

A small trickle of blood is tracing down from the corner of Alice's mouth, and her tongue comes out to clean it off—or taste it. She stares down at Mike's unconscious—I'm hoping unconscious—form and says, very calmly, "Tally-ho."

Julie has lost it. She runs over towards Mike, dropping down to her knees, sobbing openly. Her hands move towards him, pausing briefly as though held off of him by some unseen barrier, and then pushing straight through to gently cradle him.

"Why? You bitch!" she shouts up at the woman.

"I do apologize, Mrs. Newmark, but it was of vital importance that we get inside your home." She glances around briefly. "And it is a lovely home, by the way. Very tasteful."

"I agree," Alex chimes in from behind me. "They have a wonderful sense of the French Provincial working in the kitchen. It makes me wish they had carried it through the whole home."

"Oh, but that can be rather expensive, not to mention somewhat, well, tiring," Alice says right back to him.

"Very true, but if done right it—"

"Would you two shut the hell up!" It would seem that I've had enough. "You two are just...." I close my eyes tightly and notice that I can only see red in the darkness. "If you're going to kill me, just go ahead and do it. Leave them alone."

The reply I get comes from much closer than I expect.

"I assure you that I would absolutely hate to do anything to Mrs. Newmark. With her current condition, and the world's distinct lack of women with the courage to take the step that she has taken, any action against her would be tragic."

When I open my eyes, Alice is standing less than an arm's reach away. The size and warmth of the smile on her face brings a burning sensation into my throat.

"Good. Then get it over with." I think about spitting in her face, but I don't want to take the chance of changing her mind about Julie and Mike.

"Of course, we can't exactly leave them here, either. Witnesses and such," Alex says from behind me.

"You said you weren't going to—"

"Which means we'll have to take them with us, as well," Alice interrupts me sharply.

There were a couple of words there that didn't make sense.

"Take them? Take them where?"

"With you, of course," she answer with a slight toss of her ponytail.

"With me? Wait, you aren't going to kill me?"

"No, Miss Cole. My partner and I are Handlers, and we've been assigned to you, which means that we are taking you into protective custody."

"Yes," Alex continues from behind me, "we've got to get you back to the labs so that you can continue your work. This time with no annoying distractions."

"Indeed. You are far too valuable to even consider killing at this time, Miss Cole. You're perfectly safe, I assure you." Alice jostles her head, like she was telling me that I won second place at a beauty pageant or something.

I glance over at Mike and Julie, letting ideas race through my mind. "You can't take them. Mike's a cop. If he doesn't show up in the morning, then you'll have a real problem."

"Well, actually, we do have a couple of options there," Alex says.

"Yes, let's go over those, shall we?" Alice continues.

"We can call in to his supervisor and inform him that Mike has been brought in to a special investigation being conducted by the government, and that he will be temporarily re-assigned to work directly with us. Our credentials list us working for the Zombie Control Task Force, and being an expert in dealing with select zombie outbursts, he would naturally be an asset," Alex explains. "We can have the official paperwork to his precinct first thing in the morning."

"Or," Alice draws my attention back to her, "we can go through with the very unpleasant option of disposing of both Officer and Mrs. Newmark right now, and then call into the police and explain how we saw you fleeing this building in a rather unsettled state." She takes a deep breath and nods. "Which would be a good way to make sure that you don't try to go talking to the authorities again, but, as I said, I really admire Mrs. Newmark and what she's doing for our country right now, as well as Officer Newmark's service, so I would prefer the first option."

The chill that has filled the room is almost unmeasurable.

"You're both monsters," I mutter, barely audible to myself. "Inhuman monsters."

"No, Miss Cole," Alice's smile is positively beatific, "we're government employees."

Chapter Twenty

There is a faint echo off the walls right after I tap on the glass. Not surprising, really. Glass isn't exactly known for its noise dampening qualities.

Four glass walls, a glass ceiling, and a reinforced concrete floor. Unfortunately, I know this room far too well. I only got a chance to work in it that one time, but I was there for its construction, so I'm very familiar with how well put together it is. This is currently my new home, and it is anything but comfortable.

The array of cameras staring down at me don't help my mood, either. It's not that I have a sensation that I'm being watched, it's that I know for a fact that I'm being watched. No matter where I go in the chamber the cameras are set up in such a way to allow a full-body view of me in all my glory.

Not my naked glory, thankfully. I've still got most of my clothes, though they did take everything else that they felt might be dangerous, including all my jewelry, my belt, and my shoes. I'm assuming they felt that it was somehow dangerous to me, because I'm not exactly going to beat on someone with a pair of tennis shoes. Seriously, who does that?

There are other things that are definitely lacking from this chamber, too. Like a chair or bed of any sort, or even a blanket. They are keeping the room at a pleasant enough temperature, though, so at least there is that.

My eyes wander through the room for the countless time since they dropped me here, briefly lingering on the touch pad that used to have my id coded into it. I've already tried it five or six times with no luck. Still, what the hell. It's only a few steps to the door, and I put my palm flat on the reader, and…nothing. With a sigh, I turn and do one more lap around the perimeter.

There is no clock of any sort in this room or the chamber beyond, at least not right now, so I can't be sure of how long I've been here, but based on the fact that I've slept once and they've fed me twice, I'm guessing it's less than two full days. And in that time, not a single familiar face. The people bringing the food have brought it to the antechamber, let me in to get it, leave once I've stepped out of that room, and then come back for a reverse of that procedure an hour later.

The chamber outside mine is pretty much the same that I remember. Larger, plain, surrounding me completely with only a table and a set of chairs in a couple of places. Well, there are all the cameras, too, but I really try not to think about them.

I have no idea where Julie and Mike are at, or their current condition, but if I don't get some answers soon, then I'll…just have to wait until I can, actually. Right now I don't have many options.

The sound of the door opening in the outer chamber is barely audible through the glass walls of my room, but I hear it and turn just in time to see it close behind the figure who just walked inside. I recognize him instantly—it's the older man I met in the lobby, the one who was with the danger twins right before this latest mess started.

"Hello, Ms. Cole." There is the slightest tinge of joy in his voice. It's just enough to piss me off a little bit more.

I just stare at him. Well, glare is probably a better word, but I'm honestly trying to hold that back and work up to it in a few minutes.

"I do hope that you are doing well."

Wow. He managed to push me over the edge in only two sentences. That's pretty impressive, actually.

"How the hell do you think I'm doing? I'm locked in a damn glass cage, while you guys stare at me constantly! What the hell?" I use my hands as much as my mouth to communicate my point.

"I know. I'm sorry. I really didn't want this to happen this way," he states.

"Really? How did you want it to happen?" And then it occurs to me. "Wait a second, YOU'RE the one that wanted this to happen?!"

"Well, no. Not…not exactly. It's rather complicated." He turns away and takes a couple of steps. I'm not sure what I was expecting, but it wasn't that.

"Don't make me say it." I won't, dammit. I won't.

"I'm actually not that different from you, Ms. Cole. Neither one of us wanted to be where we are today, and we both have the exact same reason for it," he says with a sigh.

"Oh, you're here because of Hansel and Gretel, too?" The laugh that comes after couldn't be helped.

Him laughing was a bit of a surprise, though. "Alice and Alex? Actually, yes. They are my…Handlers…as well."

"Handlers. Yeah, they told me that name, too. What a nice term for them. A pair of sociopaths like them need a good title, I suppose."

He stands there in silence, staring at me through the glass. I'm not sure if he's waiting for me to say something more, or for him to figure out the right thing to say to me. I decide to take the initiative.

"Who are you, anyway? What do they want with you?" I ask.

He takes a deep breath, and I realize that I just started a long conversation.

"My name is Dr. Vincent Zacek, and…well, I'm afraid all of this is my fault," he sighs.

"You already said that. Well, not the name part, but the other part." I lean against the glass, settling in for the duration.

"No, I didn't mean," he waves at my cage, "this. I meant," his hands go wider, gesturing in a huge circle, "this. Everything. All of the…all of our problems."

My vision blurs slightly as my eyes narrow tightly. "All of everything what?"

His shoulders drop slightly and he looks me square in the eye. "The zombies, Ms. Cole. I'm responsible for creating the zombies."

My legs straighten and I pull myself off of the wall. Thousands of thoughts race through my brain as his words settle. For the past few years I've had questions that I couldn't answer. Puzzles that had no solution. So, finally, I ask him the only real question I could think of.

"What?"

"It was an accident, you see. A tragic one to be certain, but an accident nonetheless." When someone says something like that, you sort of expect there to be a bit of remorse in his tone. Expectations aren't always reality.

"You're going to have to say a little more than that, Doc. An accident? That doesn't quite cut it. Are you some mad scientist playing god? You know, trying to create life on your own or bring back a beloved family member or something?" Let's get to the point here!

"Actually, no. I'm a cognitive behavioral scientist who was working for one of the world's largest advertising agencies." The little nod at the end of his sentence really drives his point home.

My head shakes back and forth violently for a moment. "What? Wait, say that again? Start over, in fact."

He takes another deep breath. "Several years ago I was hired on by The Chow Agency, a firm handling some of the largest clients on every continent on the planet. Their headquarters is located in Hong Kong, but they have several offices here in the States as well, including their American headquarters in Minneapolis.

"They were looking for a cognitive scientist to work on developing a means to more directly influence their target audience. I was actually recruited directly by Heng Zhou, the current head of the company and daughter of the man who formed the company, Heng Zhou. Ah, yes, they have the same name. That's not important.

"Her plan—well, more an idea—was to come up with a means to actually physically stimulate the person experiencing the advertisement, to the point where they actually had a true need to purchase the product."

My eyes bug out and I lean my head forward a little.

"I know, I know, but as strange as it sounds, there was a certain appeal to it. From a scientific view, I mean. The team she had put together was filled with some amazing talent and brilliant minds. What we came up with was basically an enzyme that could be inserted into, well, almost anything really. Food, water, even airborne if the conditions are optimal. And then, once the enzyme was in the system, certain stimuli would activate it and create that physical need to purchase the product," he explains.

It's my turn to take a deep breath.

He continues, "Our testing began in a small suburb of Minneapolis called Woodbury. Very typical place, actually, and it fit our needs to a tee. Through means that I won't bring into question, we were able to put the enzyme in the local water supply, and then, a month later we began our test. Outdoor advertising—billboards, bus signs, and all that sort—were placed around the area advertising a new soft drink that actually didn't exist. We wanted to judge the demand for something that could only be traced to the ads and nothing else."

There is a slight smile on his face. "It was a success. A huge one, in fact—and more so, even. The thing about water is that it really does get everywhere. A groundskeeper watering the lawn at a cemetery is just one example." His eyes close. "I don't know how, but something in the enzyme was able to…to activate the primal portion of the dead. The base instinct that exists below the brain. It only worked on those who had been dead a short while, but that was enough."

He shakes his head before continuing. "Remember what I said about it going airborne? Well, it turns out that this was the perfect situation for it to travel to the dead. It spread out of control, and before we knew it…." He sighs. "Well, you know what happened."

My lips close tightly and I swallow hard. I'm not sure if I'm breathing deeply or very shallow, but I can tell that it's not a normal pattern. "Are you telling me," my words come out slowly, "that everything that is happening," but they get a little faster, "everything that has happened," and a little louder, "is because of A FUCKING MARKETING SCHEME?"

He recoils. "That seems a little simplistic."

"Are you kidding me?" Yep, I've lost it. "What the hell? Seriously, what the hell?"

"Ms. Cole, I would ask you to keep your voice down, please." His voice is somewhat stern and controlled.

Mine isn't. "Sure! Let's keep this quiet. After all, we wouldn't want anything BAD to happen, now would we?"

"Ms. Cole…."

"It's not like I'm locked in a goddamned cage—no, let's call this what it is, a cell. I'm in a damned cell, imprisoned for…. Why am I imprisoned again? I think I missed that point."

"Ms. Cole…."

"And for some reason you want to come in here and tell me about the way that you screwed up the whole world, which I have to tell you didn't really do much to improve my mood. But hey, we wouldn't want me to be in a pleasant mood, would we? After all, I'm just some woman that's been put on display. Come see the amazing nobody important! For a limited time only!"

"MS. COLE!"

I jump back and feel my body flush slightly. The good doctor can get rather loud when he wants to, it seems.

"To begin with," he returns to his normal voice, thankfully, "I would prefer you keep this quiet. Believe it or not, it isn't widely known around this facility exactly who I am and what happened to bring all of this about. So, yes, please do keep it down for everyone's security."

He's waiting for me to give him some sort of response, but I'm not up to that yet, so I just stand there staring at him.

"And I told you what I did for a very good reason, actually. For the same reason that you are here right now." He takes a small step closer to my cage. "I believe that you might be the answer for all of this."

"All...all of what?" There is barely enough volume to my voice to make it through the glass, but apparently barely is good enough.

"The zombies. The plague," he answers softly.

"Me? How? I don't…. That's ridiculous. What can I do?" I'm back to a normal volume myself.

"Because you are the only living being that we've been able to find who has been able to connect with them," he answers.

"I've already been told something like that, but I don't see how it will help. You're the scientist. In fact, since this is some kind of weird enzyme, why not just come up with another enzyme to eat that one or something. However enzymes work."

He sighs. "Well, firstly, they don't work like that. Secondly, we've tried to do the type of thing you're talking about. Many, many times, in fact. Nothing has worked."

"Okay, yeah that…that makes sense. I'm guessing that you would have started there," I answer.

"And there is one other problem." He takes another deep breath. "Shortly after the events that brought about the reanimation sequence, there was an investigation launched, and almost immediately the government tracked everything back to my lab. They even gave it a wonderful title. The Post Iatromelia Zacek Zombie Apocalypse—or P.I.Z.Z.A. for short." Did he just say pizza? As in, the same pizza that Terry has nightmares about? "It's my personal belief that the government wants an acronym for everything. I wonder what the name of the organization that comes up with acronym titles is called?" He gestures over his shoulder casually. "Anyway, once they located me I was brought to a special holding facility. That's when I first met Alice and Alex."

"The government. Our government." No dummy, he's talking about the government of the moon. Of course it's our government. "They captured you?"

"Yes. They swept in and before I knew what happened everything and everyone that I knew were gone. I was taken off to begin my new task in life."

"Getting rid of the zombies," I say with a nod.

His chuckle is a rather disturbing response. Mostly due to the fact that there is no smile anywhere near his face when he does it.

"No. Destroying the zombies has been placed far on the back burner." Now he smiles, but it is not a pleasant thing. "I've been assigned the task of controlling them."

"Controlling them?" This doesn't sound good. In fact, it sounds the very opposite of good. "Why would you want to…."

"Yes. The government wants to be able to use them for their own purposes. Now, as I understand it, there are other teams working on controlling the enzyme itself for the purpose of destroying and, sadly, creating the zombies themselves." He shakes his head. "That's not my job. My job is to find a way to control them by any means possible."

This room sure did get cold all of a sudden. "And you think that's me. That I'm the control you've been looking for."

"Something to that effect, yes."

My tongue takes a short trip across my lips, leaving them wet enough for me to talk clearly. "You have got to be kidding me."

"I'm not." He turns and walks along the glass. "My plan was actually to bring you in all along, but my Handlers wanted to take a more direct approach. Once we got you here all was going well until…." He stops and looks at me. "You know the rest."

"You didn't even think about—oh, I don't know—asking me?" I give him that wide-eyed, mouth-open, amazed-at-what-I'm-hearing look.

"You've never worked for the government before, have you?" His raised eyebrow counters my look perfectly.

There's a rather chilling thought behind that statement. "Are they…are they going to be doing anything to me? Anything like they did to Curly?"

"Who's Curly?" he asks.

"The zombie that you have splayed open on a table in the next room."

"Ah." He pauses. Don't pause. This is not a good time to pause. "Not if I have anything to say about it."

I nod back at him. "And just how much control do you have over things?"

The smile he puts on is warm, but very uncomfortable on his face. "I'm doing everything I can."

"I feel so much better." My voice is as flat as pre-sliced American cheese.

We stare at each other for a full moment—however long that actually lasts. Eventually, he gives me a slow nod.

"Well, I wanted to come talk to you. Give you an idea what was going on around here before...things happen."

"You'll pardon me for not saying thank you," I reply. He turns away and takes two steps before I stop him. "Hey! What about Julie and Mike? They have nothing to do with this. What's going to happen to them?"

He doesn't even turn back. Once again his feet start moving him towards the door. In less than a minute, I'm alone again. Naturally.

A thousand or more thoughts run through my mind, carefully pushing me towards fear and panic. The only thing that's keeping it from happening is the absolute overwhelming sensation of it all. I look around my cage—my cell—and slowly begin to take in the amazing amount of nothing that is around the room, perfectly contrasting the avalanche of possibility that was just leveled upon me.

I think about Julie. And about Mike. Then, for some reason, I think about Terry, and get mildly upset that he hasn't even come by to see me yet. And about Didi, and Dave back at the F.O.O.D.Z. station, and about going out to a bar, and...and about everything.

My eyes level up to look into one of the cameras, it's unblinking gaze staring right back down on me. There is someone on the other side of it watching my every move. Making sure that I behave.

It's at that moment that I say the only thing that I really could at that moment. Shouting it out to the people on the other side of the lens.

"You could at least have put me in a room with a damn toilet!"

I turn around, fall back onto the wall, and slowly slide down to sit on the floor. It seems that I have a lot to think about.

Chapter Twenty-One

I feel like I've been here before.

Big glass cage. A handful of zombies. Me in the cage with the zombies. Yep, that sounds awfully familiar.

What isn't the same are the people involved. Instead of the very pleasant duo of Roger and Demarius, I have Dr. Zacek and his amazingly horrible—though intolerably pleasant—accompaniment of Alice and Alex, whom I'm currently calling The A-holes. There are also three other people whom I've never met, and have no idea what to call, and ultimately I'm fine with that. They don't want to know me? Fine. I don't want to know them, either.

Okay, that might be a little childish. Still, this is the third day of this, fifth day in this cell overall, and all they've done is throw me in a room with a group of undead, giving me no idea what they want or what has been going on with the zombies beforehand.

Granted, they did finally move me to a better personal cell during my off duty hours, but as the saying goes, a gilded cage…yada yada yada. I am grateful that the new one has a bathroom at least.

"So, no clues to give me today?" I say it a little loud, knowing that they likely have the cage wired for sound anyway. Hopefully it is at least a little annoying.

Sadly, I get no answer. Oh, they say something, but I have no idea what it is. They have put sound baffles of some sort on the outside of my cage, making it almost impossible to hear what is happening on the other side of the glass without sound equipment.

So, I turn my attention to my roommates. Five of the most fragrant friends I've ever imagined. At least they don't talk much. Oh sure, there is an occasional groan, and I think one of them mumbled something about "crueler" a few minutes ago—I'm just hoping that they are addicted to crullers and my hearing was bad. The last thing I need is to discover that this group is a bunch of sadist zombies.

Four males and one female. Seems like there are always more male zombies. Maybe more women just like to be cremated, so there were less bodies to come back. It would make sense. I have yet to meet any woman who is completely satisfied with her body, so they probably wouldn't want it to be seen when they were dead, either.

In any case, I have these five here now, and I'm assuming that the folks outside the glass are wanting me to make them do a trick or something.

"You know," I shout again, "it would really help if you told me what you wanted. That way maybe I could—oh, I don't know—do something that will get me out of this damned cage!"

Nothing. I don't even turn around to look at what they are doing, because I can picture it in my head. Two of the nameless lackeys are scribing something into their e-tablet, while the other one is bustling around the room carrying one thing or another. And the good doctor and his pair of psychotic pals are still talking about something. I have no idea what that something might actually be, but sometimes it makes Dr. Zacek agitated and animated, while other times it makes him seem very dejected and disappointed—and there are times when he seems perfectly calm.

The A-holes? They always have the same reaction and expression. They are happy and smiling and way, way too polite for my taste. Seriously, I've seen Dr. Zacek all but throw things at them and all they do is smile and nod and occasionally point my way.

Now my roommates on the other hand are always exciting. Walking back and forth, always looking for something that they can't find—if they have any clue what it might be. The tallest one, a zombie with blond hair—I call him Phil, because why not—will look my way from time to time. I've waved and talked and even once did a little dance, but it hasn't done a damned thing. We've been doing this same routine for the past three days.

So, I casually put my hand back up on the exit sensor for, oh, I'm guessing the fifteenth time today, and, of course, nothing happens. I knew it wouldn't. The folks outside knew it wouldn't. Hell, Phil knew that nothing was going to happen, but that doesn't mean I'm not going to try again in a few minutes.

Or at least I would have.

The door behind me opens rather suddenly, launching me towards Phil in a rather awkward manner. Fortunately, I don't go far enough to actually encounter him, but I do move close enough that he turns towards me expectantly. My wits come back around me and I'm able to put on the brakes and drop back a step, which seems to be enough to make Phil happy. He turns away from me, and I follow suit, turning away from him and back to the door.

"Okay, Ms. Cole, we think you've done enough for the day, so it's time to go back to your room." Alice's chipper tone is enough to make me want to go back to Phil—almost.

She takes a step back, giving me enough room to move past her, which I do without even giving her a second glance. Or a single word, for that matter. I exit the room just in time to see Dr. Zacek step through the door with his three fellow white coats, but there's Alex waiting for me with a big smile.

"You did great today, Ms. Cole," he says in a sing-song voice. "Dr. Zacek feels we learned a lot from what transpired."

"Uh-huh." Dammit! That's more than I meant to say to him.

"We're going to take you back to your quarters now. They should be bringing you dinner shortly," I hear Alice say behind me as the familiar sound of the glass sealing hits me. "I hear its salisbury steak. Don't you just love a good salisbury steak?"

Somehow I manage to glare at her without ever turning around.

"I love salisbury steak," Alex states as he turns and takes his first step to guide me along. Like a good prisoner, I move in right behind him.

"I know you do, Alex," she answers from behind me. "I've got to tell you a secret, I asked for them to make that dinner. I knew it was one of your favorites."

"You must be joking!" He turns his head and looks past me. I just keep on walking. "You are way too good to me, Alice."

"I could say the same thing in reverse, you know!"

They both laugh. I take in a breath. Hold. Exhale.

"What's one of your favorite dinners, Ms. Cole?" Alex asks me without turning around.

My mouth stays completely shut. There is nothing but silence for a few seconds as we walk down the hallway.

"Oh, come now, Ms. Cole," Alice starts, "you were so very talkative back in the test chamber. Why not talk to us now?"

The list that instantly runs through my head is staggering.

"We did do you some favors you know," she continues. "You wanted a new room and we got it for you. It's comfortable and clean, and it even gives you a little privacy."

Okay, that one causes me to turn around with a raised eyebrow. There are more cameras in that room than are placed around the damned chamber behind us.

"By that she means there aren't glass walls," Alex clarifies. "You don't want just anyone staring at you as they walk on past, do you?"

"Oh, I can't imagine that anyone would want something like that happening," Alice adds.

"Not at all. And you have to be happy with the furniture selection. After all, we based it on what we found in your apartment," he states, and I swear he adds just a tinge extra glee to his voice.

And that's when I finally speak.

"You've got to be kidding me! You went back to my apartment?"

"No! Not at all," Alice says from behind me. "We took pictures the first time we were there."

"For security reasons," he tacks on.

Breath in. Hold. Exhale. "Do you really think that just adding some pleasant design to the room is going to make me happy? I'm a goddamned prisoner!"

"Now, Ms. Cole," Alice has the tone of someone chiding me for a bad joke, "would you rather be back in the test chamber? With no bed, no furniture, and as you pointed out, no bathroom?"

I'm pretty sure I growl, but I don't say a damned thing. We're getting too close to my room to waste words.

"I thought so," she teases—I think.

"When do I get to see Julie and Mike?" I decide to change the subject. Talk about something I want to know.

"We're working on that," Alex answers. "I'm really hoping that something can come together to bring us to a mutually satisfactory solution in the very near future."

"Uh-huh." I meant to say it that time.

"You sound skeptical, Ms. Cole," Alice says. "I do hope that we are able to change your attitude towards us in the near future."

"It's possible," I tell her, "there is always a chance that my opinion of you could go down."

Alex stops, and I stop right behind him. Even though I don't see her, I can feel Alice looming behind me.

"I do hope you re-evaluate us." I can feel Alice's breath on my neck. "We're only here for your safety and protection, after all. You wouldn't want anything bad to happen, would you?"

Without meaning to, I take a small step forward. My eyes meet with Alex's and I half nod towards the door to my room. He pulls his key card out from his waistband and flashes it in front of the lock. The light changes from red to green and I step forward and grasp the handle.

Before I can open it, Alice speaks, "We'll be by with your dinner in a little while. We're here to take care of you, after all. Try to relax until then, Ms. Cole."

"How comforting," I mumble as I turn the handle and step into my room.

One step inside, and I shut the door behind me, hearing the mechanized lock fall into place. I glance around the room, and as much as I hate to admit it, I feel a weight leave my shoulders when I see familiar surroundings.

My feet shuffle across the carpet, dropping off both shoes before I reach the couch. I'm barely able to turn around before I simply flop down onto the cushions. My head lolls backwards against it and I close my eyes, briefly imagining that I'm back in a much happier place and time.

Part of me is even able to imagine having Terry there to comfort me right now.

"Hi, Cici."

Yeah, that's what he would say. Something simple like that. And that wasn't my imagination, was it?

I open my eyes and Terry is standing in front of me, with that amazing, stupid, charming smile on his face. Instantly, I'm standing up, staring straight at him.

A moment later, I'm screaming and leaping right for his throat.

Yeah, it's good to be home.

Chapter Twenty-Two

They actually did put some really nice carpet in my new room. Understandably they kept the color very neutral, but they didn't just go for builder's grade. Granted it's only a step above that, but they could have played it cheap and just put anything on the floor. What's more important is that they didn't skimp on the padding. A lot of people don't realize that, in many ways, the padding is more important than the carpet. It's the carpet that shows the wear-and-tear, but it's the padding that you feel with every step. It's the thing that makes the carpet feel luxurious rather than just like a normal floor.

It's also probably the reason why there is nothing more than a soft thud issuing out every time I drive Terry's head into the floor.

"…Ci…"

Thud.

"…Ci…"

Thud.

"…stop…"

Thud.

"...please!" His hands shoot up and grab ahold of mine, which was, of course, inevitable. Which is exactly why I have two handfuls of hair, and I use that to my advantage. He might be able to stop me from driving him down, but I can sure as hell twist some hair.

"Ow! Ow! Ow!" And that is exactly the response that I was hoping to get.

"Why should I stop?!" That sounded more like a growl than me talking. "Give me one good reason to stop!"

"I love you!" he shouts up at me.

The pulling on his hair stops, but I'm hoping that he can feel every degree of the burning gaze I'm giving him right now. "You take that back!" I snarl.

"No."

There it is. One word and it's got me stuck in my tracks. I want to spit on him. Maybe pound his head back into the carpet one or two or seventeen more times. Instead, I let go of his hair—with one last shove back onto the carpet, of course. I roll off him and stand up, but I stay right over him, my foot at the ready should he do something I don't like.

"What the hell are you doing here, Terry?"

"I wanted to come check on you. Make sure you were okay." There is a nervous tremor in his voice, and I think I'm the cause.

My breathing becomes more than slightly labored for a moment. "Oh, that's just.... I'm just about ready to start pounding your head into the carpet again."

"I'm totally serious, Cici. I wanted to be here sooner, but they wouldn't let me." He's talking really fast right now. "You don't know how bad I feel about all this."

"How YOU feel?" I feel my temperature rise.

"I'm not…." He raises his hands, but with his palms out towards me. "There is no way that I can know what you're feeling, Cici. No way at all. All I want is just to make sure that you're okay. I wish…I wish I could change what happened."

There is something in his voice. A tone that just…. I step back, giving him space.

"What the hell did happen, Terry?" There isn't much volume to my voice, in any sense of the word. "Did you do this to me?"

"What? No! No, I swear I had nothing to do with this!" He jumps up to a sitting position, with just a touch of desperation showing.

"Then what did you do? I have a hard time believing that all of this is just some coincidence." I can't look at him. I won't look at him.

"Okay, I told them about you. I won't lie about that. After everything you told me, and what is going on around here, I just…I told them. I did that." There is the sound of him shuffling around, not quite moving to his feet but no longer sitting. I'm still not going to look. "I did not do this. I fought against this. I swear."

I take a deep breath, and then I look at him. He's on his knees in front of me. "But you knew. You knew about those…those… people! The A-holes! You knew who they were and you didn't say a damn thing to me!"

Don't do it, Cici. Just don't.

215

"I didn't know they were coming over to your apartment. I swear. The first time I knew about it was when you told me, and even then I wasn't sure until I came to work the next day."

"That's…that's just timing. You could have told me the next day. You could have told the police, or…or something!" I feel the first hint of water swelling at the corner of my eyes.

"I didn't know what to do. They told me it was a misunderstanding. That they just wanted to talk to you. Ask some questions. This is…this is way past anything. I didn't know, I swear."

"Stop saying that!" I scream. Why not? Why the hell not? "What is it you swear? What? Is there anything that you hold high enough to actually swear on it? You don't believe in anything, so just stop with that. Just…just stop!"

My cheeks are soaked. At some point the dam broke and my eyes decided to expose me for the terrified woman that I am right now.

And he's just kneeling there, head down, saying nothing.

"Why are you here, Terry?"

He looks up at me and for a moment I think that maybe he's the fragile one. "I don't know. I just want to help."

"And how are you going to do that?"

"I want to get you out of here." Did I hear him correctly?

"I beg your pardon?" Might as well confirm it.

He gathers his feet under him and then slowly rises up to his full height. "I'm going to get you out of here, Cici."

"H-how?" I whisper. "Do you have a plan?"

"I...don't. No." He takes a step towards me, and I react with a half-step back. "But we'll do something. Maybe just make a run for it."

"That's the stupidest idea I've ever heard." We both turn at the sound of the new, but familiar, voice.

"Ms. Dunn?" She steps out of my bedroom.

"How long were you in there?" Terry asks.

"About ten minutes longer than you were here," she answers and then turns to me. "Hello, Cici. Are you holding up okay?"

Yeah, I'll answer that later, another question is too big in my mind right now. "Wait a second. How long have either of you been here? And how did you get in?"

"I have access to everywhere in this facility," Ms. Dunn states. "They haven't thought to take that clearance away from me. Granted, I haven't given them a reason to...yet."

She and I both turn towards Terry. "I made a deal with the maid," he admits. "I bribed her."

My eyebrow goes up. "I have a maid?"

"No, there is a cleaning service that comes into your room while you are working with Dr. Zacek," Ms. Dunn explains. "We don't hire maids."

"You know what I meant," Terry huffs out. "Whatever you want to call her, I bribed her to let me into your room. I've been waiting for about twenty minutes."

"Okay. It's only a little creepy, but I'll take a little creepy over the rest of what's happening any time." My eyes go back and forth between them. "Actually, I can almost understand why Terry is here, but why are you here, Ms. Dunn?"

"Do I really come across that coldly?" she sighs. "There are many things that I do allow to happen in this facility, but I will have no part in kidnapping and imprisonment of an innocent." The smile that she puts on seems almost sweet. It's kind of disturbing. "Like Mr. Stone, I came here to check on your condition."

"But you aren't willing to break her out," Terry says.

So much for that smile. "Did I say that, Mr. Stone? I don't believe I did. There was a statement in regards to what I considered a rather foolish plan of action, however."

"Do you have a better suggestion?" He steps up to her. It's a bit of a shock, but in a good way.

"At the moment, no," she sighs softly. "We are on a time table, however. Whatever is going to be done, it must be done soon."

Oh, that doesn't sound good. Statements like that are usually followed up by revealing a ticking time bomb or something. I'm not sure I want to know what she's talking about.

"Why's that?" Yet I ask her that question, despite my better judgment.

She looks me square in the eye. "In five days they are sending in a team to extract you from this facility. They feel that this situation is too close and personal for you. They plan to move you to a new location for further study." Her head shakes slowly from side to side. "If that happens, I fear you may never be free again."

"What about Julie and Mike?" I ask.

Her head pulls back slightly, as though I slapped her across the cheek. "They are fine. As far as I know, they will be free once you are away." The composure that I have seen from her since the day we met returns quickly. "That is, again, as far as I know.

I would not be surprised if they were taken away as a tool to keep you in line."

"No. No, no, no. I can't have that. I won't be responsible for that." My hands come up to cover my face. "All of this is my fault. If I had just stood there and done my job instead of…." I can't even finish my own thought.

A gentle touch lowers my hands away, revealing a kind face staring at me. "Cici, it's not." Terry's voice caresses my fears, somehow softening them. "If anyone is to blame, it's me."

Oh yeah, he's right.

My eyes narrow. "Yeah, and I haven't forgiven you yet."

He takes a big step backwards. And then he smiles. "Wait, did you say yet? Does that mean you're going to forgive me?"

"I haven't decided."

"The two of you can have your spat later. Right now we all want the same goal—to get Cici to safety," Ms. Dunn chimes in to break the mood.

"Well, I don't know how," Terry states. "They have cameras and guards that do a regular sweep of the hallways. I had to study for two days before I could figure out how to get in here safely. To get out of here would take a lot more than the three of us."

"Wait a second, aren't there cameras in here?" I scan from corner to corner looking at the odd shapes placed in each one. "That's what those are, right?"

"No," Ms. Dunn says. "Those are fake cameras to keep you thinking you are under surveillance. I insisted that you have some degree of privacy. Surprisingly, Dr. Zacek agreed."

"He did?" I'm not sure I meant to sound so surprised.

"Apparently he thinks that having a degree of time alone will allow you to interact with the zombies more efficiently."

"Yeah, because that's gone so great," I mumble.

"Don't worry, Cici," Terry says softly. "For what it's worth, you are amazing with them. I've never seen anything like it."

I laugh. Out loud, even. "Yeah, I'm great."

"At least they pay attention to you!" he snaps back. "They don't respond to me at all. I've been trying to get anything from them. Yesterday I was trying to get this zombie to pay attention to me, and when he started walking towards me at the door I thought I had something. Then he raises his hand up, and naturally, I raise mine, thinking that we are having a moment—which kind of sounds weird now that I say it out loud." He shakes his head. "Anyway, he just walks up and puts his hand next to the door and stands there. I don't think he saw me at all."

There's that annoying burning sensation again. "Did you just complain about you not being able to spend quality time with zombies?"

"No! I mean…." I watch the panic set in on his face once more, but my mind is already traveling away. His words go through my head a second time.

"Wait, did you say that he put his hand next to the door?" I ask.

"Uh, yeah." Now he looks confused. I can understand that.

"Was this by any chance a tall zombie with blond hair?" My lower lip gets sucked into my mouth in anticipation.

Just watching his eyes I know his answer, and it's the best news I've gotten all day. "How did you know that?"

My head starts bobbing up and down in a constant nod as my mind goes to work.

"What is it, Cici?" Ms. Dunn asks.

"Well, it depends, I—" Wait a second. I look her directly in the eye. "You're calling me Cici again."

"Yes, I am," she replies with a smile.

"So, we're not at work any more?"

She smiles again, and this one is okay. "I don't see how we could be." I smile back. "Oh, and it's okay if you truly want to call me Didi. It's the least I can give you."

"Really?" My voice rises up.

"Yeah, really?" Terry echoes, with way more surprise in his voice than mine.

She turns to look at him. "Not for you, Mr. Stone."

"Why don't I get—"

"You were about to say something, Cici?" Didi cuts him off quickly.

"Oh, yeah. It's just," I take a deep breath, "I think I know how we're gonna get me out of here."

Chapter Twenty-Three

I have no idea how we're going to do this.

That isn't to say that I don't—or rather, we don't—have a
plan in place, it's just getting everything done in such a small
amount of time, well, that's going to be tough. If what Didi told
me is accurate, and I have no reason to think that it isn't, then
less than five days from now more government types are going
to show up to ship me off to who-knows-where so that I can be
more properly controlled.

Which is kinda what got everyone into this mess to begin with,
now that I think about it.

Nevertheless, I'm on a schedule. Granted, it's not a precise
schedule, more of a list of things that I need to get done so that
I can get myself and everyone else out of this place. After that
we'll fake it. I have no idea what will happen then, but getting
that far will seem like a miracle anyway.

A few things have already been checked off. First and foremost
on that list is going ahead and being out in the open. There
is no way that Zacek and the A-holes aren't going to find out
about Terry and Didi visiting me, so the obvious tact is to tell

them directly. Which means that both of them have already—or at least should have already—gone and spoken with others regarding their time with me.

That story is pretty simple, actually. At the heart of it is the fact that Terry came to the room to apologize to me—which is true. In response, I beat his head against the floor—which is also true. Didi had come there to see me as well, making sure that there was nothing that I needed in my new room. Finding Terry and I locked in a rather unpleasant situation, she interceded and separated us. One heated debate later she left my room with Terry in tow, leaving me alone. The fallout is that Terry is a little miffed that I was so violent towards him, and Didi feels that I need more time to adjust before I can give worthwhile feedback.

So, one part down. It's just the rest of the plan that is going to be tough, and there are at least three key points that have to fall into place, or I'll be taking a nice long drive or flight or whatever it is they plan to get me wherever I'm going.

I wonder where that would be? According to everything I've read, the CZC is the leading facility for zombie research in the world. Heck, they pretty much told me that exact thing when I started working here. So, would I be moved to a second-rate facility or are they lying about this place? Maybe there is some super-secret underground facility that's disguised as a pharmaceutical company or something. That would make sense, since this is kind of a disease—an enzyme is like a virus, right? Man, I should have paid more attention in biology class.

"Ms. Cole?" Dr. Zacek's voice shocks me back to the moment. "Is there something wrong?"

There is no doubt that the expression on my face answers that question perfectly well, but since I have been sitting here on my ass for the past, well, however long I've been doing it, I'll give him a verbal response to go with it.

"Are you kidding me?" Huh, I really did plan for that to be a little more friendly.

"You seem somewhat distracted." It seems that he isn't going to bite on my prodding

It's not intentional, but I let out a heavy sigh. Then I decide to run with it. "I'm bored."

Nothing. No change in his expression at all. "I can understand that. Unfortunately, there is little that I can do to—"

"Let me walk around." We're not going down his rabbit hole. Let's take my path instead.

"You know that I can't—"

"Put a dozen people around me. Let the A-holes," I nod towards Alice and Alex, "go with us. What am I going to do? You've got my friends locked up."

He hesitates. I keep going.

"I'm not saying let me go outside. I mean just walk around the facility. Let me see something besides this room and my personal quarters." I stand up, looking him square in the eye. "I just want to, I don't know, feel like I'm at least doing something. Let me go look at the zombies that have already visited me, even. Just walk through the room."

"Ms. Cole, I—"

"Just a walk. Wait until the room is clear, even, I don't care. I just…." I force my shoulders to slump. "Dr. Zacek, just let me do something else. Please?"

He stands there, staring back at me. A small smile crosses his face, and I can see his breath move his head slightly.

"Ms. Cole...." He pauses, I think waiting for me to interrupt him. "Ms. Cole, you do understand that you are in a unique situation, don't you?" I nod. "This means that we—or at least I—have no experience with this. I promise you that I don't want to see you miserable, but, in many ways, my hands are tied. I'm as much a victim of this as you are."

I am very proud of myself for not shouting him out of the room at that exact moment. Instead, I smile softly and say, "Then don't be a victim. Help us both out by letting me just go for a walk. I'm not even asking to see my friends or other people who don't already come in here." His mouth twists into a crack, so I push right in. "When we met in the lobby, you were miserable, weren't you?"

That had an impact. "You were happy just to be away from all of this," I wave my hands around in a circle, "and I could see it in your face and hear it in your voice. All I'm asking is for that same chance. A chance to feel like I have the slightest bit of freedom, or at the very least the illusion of it."

His head drops, and my heart races. I have no idea what I look like right now, but I'm doing my damned best to make sure that I show nothing.

"No promises," he mutters.

"No!" I put my hand on the glass towards him. "No, I'm not asking for anything but a chance. I just want to...to feel like something is in my control. That I can actually go for a walk now and then."

"You do understand that anything I can do can't be guaranteed to last, either." He looks back up at me with something between concern and commitment in his eyes.

"And I would never, ever put that sort of pressure on you." No, the pressure I'm thinking of right now goes more at the base of your skull.

He smiles, and I smile right back at him. "Hopefully I can have something arranged in a few days."

Crap. "A few days!" Okay, I didn't mean to actually shout that out loud.

"Were your expecting a miracle, Ms. Cole?" he half sighs.

"No! I was hoping to go for a walk after all this." I turn around and thud my back onto the glass. Gravity takes its course, and I don't fight it, and a second later I'm sitting on my rump, my back to the good doctor and that side of the room.

"Now, Ms. Cole, you have to be understanding," he says with that tone a parent gets with their eight-year-old.

"Yeah, right," I grumble—like an eight-year-old.

"Why don't you get up and interact with some of your companions."

Oh yeah. I look up and see three zombies staring at me. Not towards me, but right at me. I would say that we lock eyes, but I really don't like staring at those milky-white husks if I can avoid it.

Still, they remind me what I'm trying to do, and why I'm trying to do it.

I spin around on the ground and rise straight up, startling the man on the other side of the glass.

"Half an hour." I say plainly.

"Half an hour what?" he replies.

"You let me go walk for half an hour, and I'll come back here and jump through your hoops. You don't give me anything, and I won't give you anything." I'm past the pleading. This is direct bargaining.

"Don't start with that attitude. If you don't work with us, then you won't be able to—"

"I don't have anything! I have nothing! What am I going to lose? Huh?" I turn and point back to the zombies behind me and then turn right back towards him. "I'm going to lose the riveting conversations that I'm having without it?" My head shakes in short, sharp turns. "Nope. I have nothing. I'm a damned prisoner, and you know it. All I want is to take a walk. A goddamned walk!"

"And I—"

"Have nothing!" I interrupt him instantly. "This isn't something that you can just bring in my understudy for, is it? I'm stuck here, I know that. Not a damned thing I could do about that, so I want my one little token. I want to walk around." I shrug. "Take it or leave it. It's that simple. I walk, or I sit."

The smile is gone. Right now all he has is a scowl, and I don't really care. I don't have the time to make friends, it seems. At least not friends like him.

He turns around and motions towards the twins and then begins walking towards them. They meet a few feet away from my cage. Too far away for me to hear what they are saying. It would be nice to be able to read lips, but frankly, I suck at that kind of thing. They are talking, though, and Doc seems to be a little animated about it.

A minute later he's walking away, leaving Alice and Alex staring at me in the cage. Then they start to walk towards me, and my instinct tries to get me to take a step back, but I swallow that annoying little thing down and stand my ground.

"Don't we have some gumption! Good for you!" Alex chimes with a sing-song tone. "It seems that you are going to go for a little walk." He wags a finger. "Not a big one. Just a little one around for a bit, but at least you'll get to stretch your legs."

"Outside this room," I counter, and I think my voice cracks slightly. "It doesn't count unless I go outside this room. Let me just walk around the pens where I used to work. Give me some degree of familiarity."

"Sure!" Alice answers. "It's always good to see something familiar and welcoming. Let's go there."

Her hand slips over the sensor outside the chamber and my door opens up. Once I've stepped inside the antechamber, the door behind me closes and the one in front of me opens.

I take a deep breath and feel a genuine smile creep onto my face.

"Oh, one more thing, though." Alice steps up to me, tossing her ponytail behind her casually. "If you do try to do something stupid, you know, like run away or something, I'm afraid I'll have to break your leg." Her nose crinkles up. "Or maybe both, really."

There isn't a doubt in my mind.

"I understand. I promise I won't try to get away. All I'll do is walk around the room and just…look at things." Damn straight I will.

"Then, we won't have any problems at all, Ms. Cole," Alex chimes in joyfully. He waves his arm wide towards the door that leads to my destination. "After you."

I take a step. And then another. And then I'm walking towards the door, and it suddenly hits me that this is really happening.

Step one is complete. Maybe this will work after all.

Chapter Twenty-Four

Sadly, the next part is out of my control. I'd like to say that at least we were able to coordinate what was happening, but if this is going to work, there can't be any sign of the three of us working together at all.

It's hard for me to decide who has the tougher job at this point. Terry's is probably more physically taxing and potentially dangerous, but Didi's has the constraint of needing precise timing. Though, honestly, the idea of Didi not being able to time things to the second sounds rather odd.

Myself, I just have to follow through with what I started, which means walking daily, and if I can, two or three times a day. And it's not just enough to walk. I have to walk the exact same places in the exact same way.

It's the third day of my walking privileges, which means that everything has to go down tomorrow morning.

Y'know, thinking on it, there is also still a chance that either Terry or Didi will bail on this plan. I want to think that they are genuine in their concern, but this is a lot of risk. If this doesn't go right, either one—or both—could end up in a worse situation than I'm in right now. And honestly, there's no doubt that I would end up in a far worse situation. Which is really scary so I don't want to think about that right now.

Anyway, this is day three, and I'm trying to keep an eye open for signs that things are going according to plan. My eyes wander around the room. Twenty or so glass cells filled with zombies of all shapes and sizes. My daily walk through the testing grounds.

This is where my part of the plan becomes the most risky. If I don't get things right here, then what Terry and Didi are doing means nothing.

"What is it, Ms. Cole?" Alex's voice startles me and I actually jump slightly.

"I…I beg your pardon?" I stammer back.

"You seem unusually nervous today. Is something wrong?" He's prying. I don't need prying. I don't need any of this. Don't throw me off. Not now.

"No. No, I was just wondering…." What? What was I wondering? "Do you call it soda or pop?" Did I really just ask that?

"Well, that's an odd question," he mutters.

"Soda, obviously," Alice chimes in, and for a change I'm glad she did.

"Soda?" Alex glance back. "No, no. I've always called it pop."

"That's because you come from the midwest. That's the only place that it's called pop. Everyone else calls it soda." She half laughs at him. Perfect.

"And that makes it wrong?" You go, Alex.

Edible Complex

While you are going, I'm going to take this chance to do a quick scan. I'm going for a headcount this time.

"Not wrong, per se, just…not right."

I wish I could mark this down. Counting like this always gets awkward for some reason. If they were consistent in the number of zombies in each room this wouldn't be so tough.

Alex lets out a snort. I honestly wasn't expecting that. "This coming from a woman from California."

"You are not saying bad things about California, are you?" There is an extra hint of nice in her question. This must be a sensitive subject.

"I would not do that," Alex says with a calm version of annoyingly happy. "Actually, I really, really like California. Some of our best times together were in California."

Halfway through the count. Keep talking you two.

"That's true. Our first case together was just outside San Francisco. Do you remember?" Alice's tone goes back to normal, which is good—I think.

"How could I forget? Back before the zombies came, which makes it all the more ironic." He laughs softly.

"You do what you have to do. Always go that extra mile!" Okay, ignore her and finish the count. Not that many more to go.

"I learned that from you," he answers. "You taught me a lot that day. I still hold it as a proud memory."

Almost there. Just three more rooms to count.

"Well, we couldn't exactly leave evidence behind, could we?" she giggles. Actually giggles.

"But what a way to get rid of it, eh?" He doesn't giggle. That's good.

Just one more room to go.

"When you have no other options, your hunger will get you through." That's right, just keep…wait, what?

"It's a shame that he was so fat, though. Not very healthy at all." He did not just suggest…

"Not every meal is going to be healthy. It's why you have to strive to make sure you do eat healthy when you can, because you won't always be able to," she says with conviction.

They can't honestly be talking about what I think they are talking about.

"I know, I know, but still. I never really knew how much fat one can have until that day. Seeing it is one thing, but experiencing it like that…." He shudders. I join him. "At least we had some of that local beer to wash it down."

"Not for me, remember? I don't drink. Though I did go through a lot of water. Lots of gristle on that one." She shakes her head. "And we were there for three days, pretty much constantly eating."

"OH MY GOD!!" I shout and cover my ears. My eyes squeeze tight and I desperately try to get the images that keep flashing in my head out of there. "You two are… AAAHHH!"

I suddenly realize exactly what I've just done. I screamed in the middle of the room and came to a dead stop, didn't I? That's probably not a good thing.

Slowly, one of my eyes pries apart, giving me a clear view of both of my companions as they stare at me quizzically.

"Are you all right, Ms. Cole?" Alice asks.

"Better than that guy the two of you killed and ate out in San Francisco!" There is bile in the back of my throat as I actually voice the words.

Both of them stare at me with blank expressions before they turn and look at each other. That's when they start laughing. Which really should be far more disturbing than it seems right now.

"We didn't eat a person, Ms. Cole," Alex says cheerfully, "we ate a person's prize bull."

"A…bull?" The word comes out of me rather haltingly.

"Yes, Ms. Cole," Alice says. "A bull. We were to send a message to a particular group of, oh heck, let's just call them bad people, and one of them was very fond of his prize bull. We killed it, and then ate it in front of him." She shakes her head with a frown. "Beef really isn't very good for you. Very fatty."

"I…" can't believe I'm saying this "…am sorry. I shouldn't have jumped to a conclusion like that. It just sounded like you were talking about actually eating a person, and I kind of freaked out." Not that what they did was really that good, though.

"Understandably," Alex answers with a laugh. "In fact, why don't we head back to your room. Let you rest a little. Calm down."

Crap, I got distracted. I'm not done. "It's okay. I'm all right," I explain. "Just taken back a little."

"No, I insist," Alice steps towards me, twisting up her face a little, and giving me that teasing glare. "You're not getting sick on my watch!"

She moves behind me, pushing me along without actually ever making contact. My eyes flash back at her, and then just past her. I lost count. I'm not sure where I stopped and what was left. Dammit! I'm not sure if it's the same number from yesterday.

"I guess I'll just say yes," I mutter, and then realize that I said it aloud.

"Yes, you will!" Wait, she thought I was answering her? "So march along, young lady! Tally-ho!"

As I turn back I see Alex looking my way. He waits until I've taken my first step before falling in line in front of me. "I'm really sorry that we upset you, Ms. Cole. We really should pay more attention to what we're saying."

"Or at least how we're saying it," Alice adds on.

"That's okay. It was just my imagination running away with me." I don't even have time to look at what the zombies are doing right now. That was going to happen on the next lap. And there's really no time for another try. I'm just going to have to hope things are the way we planned.

"Don't worry about it, Ms. Cole. Just keep performing and everything will be just fine." There's a tone to her voice that isn't normally there. An ominous sound to it. And here I thought her normal cheery tone was bad enough.

"I'm sorry. Again. It's just…." I take a deep breath and let it out slowly in a semi-sigh. "I mean, it's silly to think that you guys would…. I mean, it's just that…." I shake my head, clearing out the thought. "I can't believe I thought you ate a person. That's just ridiculous."

The silence that follows is way too long. We're already in the hall back towards my room before I say anything else.

"It's ridiculous, right?" I glance ahead to Alex and even back towards Alice. His face I couldn't see, but hers is almost glowing with a smile.

"Well, I never said that, did I?" she quips.

Ho. Ly. Crap.

Chapter Twenty-Five

Today's the day.

One way or another, something is going to happen today. I'm hoping it's to my benefit, but if it ends up being the one where I get shipped off to god knows where, then I'm betting the good part of it is out the window. Assuming wherever I end up actually has any windows.

"How are you doing today, Ms. Cole?" I look over to see Dr. Zacek standing beside the door with a broad smile on his face. The back of my mind starts to itch.

"Actually, I was just sitting here wondering that same question, Doc." My mind focuses on what might happen, and I start to stretch. I raise one arm high over my head and lean to my right, and then reverse the order casually.

"Well, you seem very spry, at least," he half-laughs. Yeah, keep laughing.

"Gotta keep in shape. I'm not as active as I used to be," I answer honestly. Even if that's not why I was saying it.

"Yes, I do understand." He takes a deep breath. Time for a lecture or at the very least a conversation. "Actually, that's one

of the things that I wanted to talk to you about." Nailed it!
"As much as I try to empathize with you, I realize there is no
way that I truly can. The more that I think about it—about
you—the more I've come to appreciate the woman that you are.
You've impressed me, Ms. Cole."

Gee, thanks. "That's very kind of you to say, Dr. Zacek." What
the hell, why not ask? "I don't suppose this is where you tell me
that you're letting me go home due to good behavior?"

"Nooooo." Great, not only a no, but the long, drawn out no.
"Not exactly, anyway. You are going to be moving, but you
won't be going home." Here it comes. "It's been decided that
you might fare better at another location. Somewhere that is
away from here and the other research that could potentially
distract from what we're trying to accomplish."

"So, I'm being sent to a different prison?" I can't help myself.
"I've heard that happens sometimes."

"Not a prison, Ms. Cole. I don't ever want you to think of
this as a prison. What you are doing is helping everyone," he
counters quickly.

"HA!" I don't laugh, I actually yell that word. "Tell me, Doc, do
you think there is any chance in hell that I will ever be able to
walk outside by myself? Go to a movie? Just…do whatever I
want?"

He pauses, and I see something move behind his eyes. "I don't
know. I hope so. For both of our sakes, actually."

"Right." The word slowly works its way out of me. I swallow
back all of the other venom that tries to work its way out of me.
"So, do you know where I'm going?"

"WE are going to be traveling to New Mexico. There is a secure
facility there that we will be using. There are actual living

facilities there, too, so—at least in theory—we will have better quarters for ourselves."

"New Mexico?" Something about that place…. Oh no. "Wait a second, are they sending me to Area 51?"

"We are being transferred to a secure facility," he repeats.

"Is it a government facility?" My voice goes up a tone or two.

"It's a secure facility." He stares at me through the glass.

"Well, I guess we'll find out when we get there, huh?" Not if I have anything to say about it. Now the tough question. "When am I leaving?"

"Official word finally came in today. The transport personnel will be here in an hour or so." An hour. That's…maybe enough time, actually.

"So, I get to have at least one more walk around the place, then?" Make it sweet. Make it nice.

"Of course. It's pretty much your normal break time now—a few minutes early, but considering the situation I don't see a problem." He motions over to a couple of people in white lab coats whom I don't recognize. "These two will go on your walk with you today. It will likely be a little more pleasant than your normal walk."

No A-holes? No complaints. My odds just went up, I think. I hope.

The door opens up and I step into my antechamber, and then move out once the other one swings wide.

"I appreciate everything that you've done, Dr. Zacek." Halfway, maybe. "I'm sure we'll get at least one more chance to talk before I get out of here today."

"No doubt. I'll be in and out of this room all day. I don't know how much more work we'll get in today, but I do hate to waste time, so…we'll see." His smile isn't something I would call warm, but it's not cold, either.

"Don't worry, Doc. We'll find each other." I turn and wave over my shoulder. "See you!"

He doesn't reply, or if he does, I don't hear him. I step up to the door, with the two white coats behind me. It takes them a minute to figure out that they have to open the door for me, since I don't have a key card at all. One swipe later, and we're moving, and then I make a bee line for the testing grounds.

A big part of me wants to break into a run, sprint to the room and get ready, but in actuality, I'm ahead of schedule anyway, so I slow down. A couple of minutes later and I'm there. Over one hundred zombies—if the count is still correct, which I'm hoping it is—stagger around their various cells. Well over a dozen of them turn to look at me as I walk in, and it brings a big smile to my face.

Behind me the two gentlemen who haven't even introduced themselves chatter away about something, but I don't really hear them. My thoughts and concentration are focused on the long walk I'm taking around the room, past as many of the individual cells as I can.

One full lap brings me back around to where I started, and I stop. My temporary handlers pause behind me as I take a moment to stretch out once more. Arms up, twist to the side, switch and repeat.

I steal a glance at the clock, noting the time. Taking a moment, I draw in a deep breath and turn around to look at my two companions. A smile creeps across my face. Might as well prepare for this like it's going to happen, right?

"Can I help you, Ms. Cole?" the first of the nameless white coats asks me, and I can't hold back a chuckle.

"No, I don't think you can, actually."

For some reason, I thought there would be a sound. A loud click or a buzz or something. Anything to add gravitas to the moment, but I guess I've seen too many movies. If anything, the only sound that I get is one of sudden dead silence—which honestly can be as unnerving as any loud sound in its own way.

The power to the room dies. The lights go out, and we are plunged into total darkness. Just like we planned.

Showtime.

Chapter Twenty-Six

One consistency that I've always kind of noticed about the dark is the fact that it is a great equalizer. In the dark, everyone is the same. We can't see each other or anything else, giving us a bit of a sense of wonder. What is nearby? Am I alone?

"What the hell?"

Of course, sound does help where vision fails in some areas. You can hear the sounds of others nearby, for example. Like if, for example, someone was escorting you on a walk through an area that was suddenly plunged into an inky blackness, making each and every one of us effectively blind.

"Don't panic, the emergency generators should kick in."

People often take steps to avoid things like total darkness, too. Though those don't always work. Especially not if others have taken actions to make sure that those backups are out of commission.

"What the hell was that sound?"

The loud clicks and growing moans from the room add another level of ambiance, as well. In the darkness, even the smallest sounds seem louder somehow, too. You might even feel like someone—or something—that is across the room is sitting right next to you.

"Oh God. Oh God, they're out. The zombies are out!"

It's pretty easy for panic to set in. The mind is much more powerful than anyone really wants to realize.

The sounds of clutter and pain roll through the room as the two men who were accompanying me only a few moments ago stumble and bumble their way through the room, moving back away from me and, they hope, towards the exit.

I suppose that I would be doing that, too, had I not spent the last handful of days walking the exact same pattern through the exact same room, memorizing my steps and counting off not only where I was, but how many zombies I could expect to be in front of or behind me at the moment of darkness.

It also kind of helps that I knew it was coming. Not the exact moment, but the approximate one, and this approximate works just fine.

Time for my first action. Let me get into character. Ahem. "Oh no! They're everywhere! They've gone mad! They're attacking! Ahhhhhh!" Yeah, that should do it.

Chaos erupts from across the room. I'm guessing that it's just the two white coats making things a little worse for themselves. After all, it wouldn't be the zombies. One of the things that I've learned—thanks to the constant talk from both Roger and Demetrius—is the theory that zombies don't actually see anything. After all, their eyes are always cloudy and many times just flat out missing. No, they "see" in some other way that we haven't figured out yet. At least that's what my two smart friends figure.

Which basically means that zombies can see in the dark. Oh, and they still have that nasty problem of reacting poorly to violence. Bump into them and you're fine, but if you run into them at full speed, well, there is a chance that they might take that as an attack, which would be bad for the other person.

I really don't want the two white coats to get hurt, so hopefully their sense of direction is pretty good. If they run straight towards the door they'll get to it safely. The sharp sound of a chair clattering to the ground gives me doubts, but I hold my position. I don't want to start moving until I know where I have to go and what I have to do. If they can just make it to that door.... The familiar sound of the exit opening across the room couldn't come at a better moment.

"Noooo!" I'm really trying to sound terrified here. And actually, I guess I am, just not for the reasons that I'm pretending. "They've got me! They've got me!"

Well, one did just walk past me. I think. I'm pretty sure I felt him—or her—brush against my arm lightly. More importantly, the two white coats hopefully believe that I'm a goner. If they do, then everything is in pretty good shape.

See, the plan is pretty simple.

It suddenly occurred to me that the zombies weren't doing what we originally thought. It wasn't a matter of eating the right thing, or teaching them what to eat, but just having something that they wanted. These weren't creatures just mindlessly moving from place to place, they were motivated. Granted, it isn't really a motivation that we understand, but they do have their own needs and wants. Food is one of those things. And from what I've seen, freedom is another.

When Phil the zombie put his hand on the glass, he wasn't doing something I told him to do, it was because he saw me doing it and somehow I got out. So, he was trying to do the same thing. He wanted out. We both were in the same situation, and we both were captives in this place. So, if that's the case, why not work together?

So, all I needed were a couple of allies. It took a little convincing, especially considering the risks that both Terry and Didi were going to have to take, but their guilt slightly outweighed their sense of self. Everyone has their jobs, and it only works if we all do them as planned.

Terry's job was to make sure that all the cell doors were set to rescue mode, as though a worker might be trapped inside, which means that during a power failure, they automatically unlock and swing open. Naturally, this is the type of thing that is rarely used, and is designed to be used on only a single cell at a time, so the idea of having every cell in the place set to spring open and release its contents at the same time wasn't something they had considered.

Then there was the matter of the power. Like my white-coated friends mentioned, there are power back-ups in place, so even during a power outage, it would only last the four or so seconds it would take for the power batteries to kick in and provide a temporary solution. Unless the director of the facility arranged for a complete overhaul of the systems, causing them to temporarily go offline. So when the power to the facility is mysteriously cut off, there isn't anything to come online. A one in a million chance, really.

And all of that was just to make sure that I was in this room when the power went out and the doors to the cells opened up. It won't take too long for someone to get the power back online. A place like this has too many redundancies to imagine it would last forever. Besides, I haven't memorized the footprint of the whole place.

You see, if I'm going to get out of here, I'm going to have to fight my way out. It's not going to be as easy as the first time.

Edible Complex

This time around I'm going to have to get past locked doors, security guards, and government employees just to make it outside, and then…. Well, okay, I haven't thought that far yet. I'm still hoping that this first part works. Still, to make it through all of the obstacles in front of me it would take an army. Fortunately, this place had one ready for me, and they just got set loose.

Now I just have to do my job, or at least the first part of my job. The doors to this room have some very secure electronic locks, so I have to make my way to the far door before the power comes back on so that the way out will be clear before the power comes back. Which is where all that counting and all those steps come in handy.

Slowly, deliberately, I walk forward, recounting each step in my head and picturing my surroundings. On my right I'm just about to pass the last of the chicken cells and move to the vegetable offerings. After that is the apple cell, and thinking on it, those poor creatures are probably still sitting there inside their glass cage waiting for the next dose of what their masters are going to feed them. I can hope, though.

And finally, on left is the live animal cells. At first we thought about leaving them alone. Not taking the chance that they would see the people in the facility as their next meal, but if we're going to make it out like all of these zombies are horrible monsters, we're going to have to deal with the fact that there actually are a few of them in the lot.

Just a few more steps and I should find…. The wall hits my outstretched hand and I immediately start following it to my right. It should only be a few more feet to the door, and thankfully, it is. I fumble around until my hands fall onto the emergency latch, and I hold my breath as I give it a turn. A loud click is the best sound I've heard all day, and I feel the door swing open.

None too soon, either. An eerie red glow fills the room as the emergency lights finally kick in. I've never understood why the emergency lights are tinted. Maybe it's just a clear way to tell them apart from the regular lights. Or maybe it has something to do with wavelength and how well you can see in the dimmer light. I do vaguely recall something about red light being at the end of the spectrum, which is why the police used to use them on their cars. Except now they use blue lights. So…oh hell, what difference does it make? The lights are red, and the room now has that lovely tint to it.

And by lovely I mean that the whole room looks like an odd snapshot from hell.

The living dead wander about, the hue of the lights giving them a fire-like, bloody appearance, and more than just a hint of scary. Fortunately, even though they look different, they are acting the same as always. Several are making their way towards each of the open doors, and it's up to me to get this going the right way.

"Hello!" I shout, even though I know that it won't do any good. Just instinct I guess. I also take a moment to jump on top of a table and wave my arms about, doing what I can to draw their eyes—or whatever it is they use to see—to me. "I know you want to get out of here. I want to get out of here, too, but…." Why the hell am I talking to them? The motion will bring them in, so I use my arms to draw their attention towards me. Get them interested.

"Now, Ms. Cole, what are you up to?" Oh crap. I know that voice. I also knew he was going to show up, I just didn't expect it to be this quick.

A turn on the table, and I'm looking right at Alex.

"Get down from there and come along. This is already a mess. Don't make it any worse." That damn tone of his. The happy, but screw-you-anyway tone that he's had since that night at my apartment.

"Not a chance in hell," I say with more than a little venom.

"I really don't want to do this the hard way, Ms. Cole. If you don't do what I say, however, well, I'm afraid that I will have to take some drastic actions." He's getting close to me. I guess this is as good a test as anything.

"Bring it on, A-hole." What the hell, I even add on the little come-at-me motion with my hand. If I'm going to do this, I might as well go all out.

"My, my! What bravado!" I swear his smile gets even bigger. "Well then. Tally-ho!"

He moves towards me and I stay perfectly still. My heart races, pounding louder and louder in my ears with every step. Reflexively, I swallow as his hand reaches out towards my ankle. An image of me falling down from this high table, crashing onto the ground and caving in my skull flashes through my head. I'll admit it, I screamed when his hand grabbed ahold of me.

Fortunately, that was the only scream that came from me.

A handful of those zombies that I had been doing my best to get the attention of responded right away. Two of them lashed out at Alex the same second I screamed, forcing him to let go of my leg.

For a second the terror remains with me, for a couple of reasons, actually. The first one because—as I should have expected—this guy can fight. I watched his female cohort take out Mike, so I shouldn't be surprised that he can hold his own. There are a couple of things going against him, though, the fact that there are a lot of zombies for him to deal with, along with that whole already-dead-so-really-hard-to-hurt-or-kill thing. The other thing that disturbs me is the vicious quality of the zombie's assault. They aren't subtle or forgiving at all.

"What the hell?" His scream takes me rather off guard. Though I can't really blame him. If I had a swarm of zombies falling on me I'd scream, too. "I didn't touch them! I know better than to touch them!"

"Yeah, you might think that," the words come out of me with a bit of a gag in my throat, "but you'd be wrong. You guys spent so much time putting me with them and having me try to get to know the zombies that you really didn't think about what that would mean, did you?" Carefully, I squat down, so that I can slide my legs off the table and then drop back to the ground. "In their opinion you did attack one of them. You attacked me."

What happens is rather gruesome. I can't say for certain that Alex was killed by them, but if he wasn't then he is going to have a lot of recovery time ahead of him. Not only were pounding blows rained down upon him, but the bony tips of exposed fingers clawed into his flesh, ripping long gashes into his clothing, and I presume his flesh as well. There was blood, I know that for certain. More blood than I ever want to see again in my life, actually.

He doesn't go down quickly or easily, but he does go down. For a second I'm fearful that the zombies might follow through and act like the ones that we've always feared—that they are going to actually consume him. They don't. Turns out they have better taste than that.

I push back my own disgust and reach over to grab his pass key. That might come in handy, after I wipe the blood off it anyway.

My arms go back into motion, drawing their attention back to me. Slowly, they all turn to face me, and I can only hope that they are paying full attention.

"Okay, you all want to get out of here, right?" Yeah, give them a pep talk. Words seem to matter a little bit, just not as much as actions. "Well, so do I, so we're going to get out of here together." I look towards the door in the distance, leading back into the heart of the facility. I can feel my tongue play across my teeth as I squint my eyes, trying for a better view.

"But we aren't going alone." I begin heading towards the door—with a pretty good size group of undead monsters walking beside me.

Chapter Twenty-Seven

I've been down this road before. Well, actually it's a hallway, but the principle remains the same. It's a familiar path, and one that I never thought I would want to walk down again. Part of me is hoping that this is a pointless venture—a complete waste of time that I could be using to get away from this place—but I think I already know better. Somewhere deep inside, I realize that I'm going to see exactly what I'm afraid to see.

The door is standing in front of me. My unliving companions are already milling about, looking for something or someone of their own. I think I've lost about ten percent of them or so just on the walk here, but that's to be expected. I want them all to get out of here with me, but I know better. Some of them are going to wander off, and I just don't have the time to play zombie wrangler.

And I'm using all of these thoughts as a distraction. It's time to do this.

My hand reaches out and I feel the cool touch of the metal in my hand. Enough so to make me realize that my palm is sweaty. Lovely. I pass the borrowed key card in front of the reader but there is no change to the light on the lock. It's blinking red at me over and over. I decided to try it anyway.

It turns with a gentle click. The backup generators that have kicked in still haven't activated all the locks I guess. Either that or they were out long enough to completely deactivate. Frankly, I don't care. All that matters is that the door swings open, and the scene inside sends a frozen spike to my heart.

He's still here. If anything he looks worse now. The image reminds me of a spider web, pulled and arranged in a particular pattern. My throat fills with my breakfast, pausing just long enough for me to force it back down. I don't think I noticed the smell before. Or maybe it's just gotten that much worse.

"Don't worry, Curly," determination takes over and I step inside, "we're both getting out of here today."

Big words, but I have no idea where to begin. Long strands of flesh have been pulled up and away, tied back and weighted down so that they can be left on the table. His organs are still beside him, resting on the cold metal slab, and all four extremities are strapped securely in place. He's still also missing the top of his skull, while a bunch of electrodes or something are sticking into his brain.

Oh, and they went ahead and added something to his one good eye, too. I'm not sure what it is. Kind of looks like a clear inverted funnel of some sort, but it sure doesn't look like something that I would want on my eyes. Hell, I freak out at the thought of people putting contacts in their eyes. And I get to remove whatever it is that is attached to Curly. Yay.

First things first. As much as I'm sure he won't like it, I'm gonna need to keep him strapped down. Otherwise he might try to get up and leave, dragging a lot of himself behind—if he could even do that. I have no idea what he would be capable of doing. The worst case that I've ever seen just had a big tear in his stomach with a little bit of his guts showing. I don't know if he could walk like this or not. Frankly, I don't want to know, I just want to get him fixed up.

And I'm going to do that how again?

I step around to the top of his head, finally getting a good look at his brain. Now there's a statement that I never imagined myself saying, yet, here I am. It's way more than I know what to do with, but the one thing I do know is that zombies are pretty damn tough, so I do the only thing I know to do: I rip out the wires. A couple of small bits of brain go with a couple of them, but for the most part they come out clean. Unfortunately, it doesn't appear that the fine folks who did this to Curly decided to leave the bit of the top of his skull nearby. I'm sure that it's somewhere being analyzed for this and that—or maybe being made into a nice paperweight for one of the sick bastards who did this. I have no idea.

What I do have are some towels that I can wrap around the top of his head, and then secure somehow. And that somehow looks like it's going to be tying it down with wires. And so, I do just that. I wrap the towel around him like he just got his hair washed, and then take the wires that I just ripped out of that same head and wrap them around his skull and then neck and then skull again until I feel that it's somewhat secure. It's a temporary fix to be certain, but it's better than nothing.

Now it's time to do something with his eye. I see my hand as it reaches towards the odd thing secured to his eyeball and it's shaking more than a bowl of jello in a car with bad shocks on a bumpy road. That kind of shaking. Okay, this is freaking me out. Maybe he can see with it on still?

I feel myself sigh more than I hear it. There is no way that I can leave that thing there. And I don't get it, because I was just messing with this guy's brain, and now I'm scared of a thing on the eyeball? Deep breath.

Trying to go on automatic, I quickly reach my hands out and grab it and pull it up. There's resistance, and an audible pop as it pulls free.

"Ew! Ew! Ew!" I'm sure the little dance that accompanies my statement helps tremendously. Throwing the suction thingy across the room is just an added bonus.

"I am very disappointed in you, Ms. Cole." I'm so used to that voice being happy and cheery that I don't recognize it at first. Sure enough, there's Alice. At the door to the room. With all the zombies outside. This isn't a good thing.

"Here we go and do favors for you," she continues, "letting you have special treatment because of how nice and cooperative you have been—or should I say, thought you had been—and you betray our trust by doing," her arms flail around slightly, "whatever this is."

Very quickly I move to place Curly and his table between me and the unhappy psycho whom I previously thought only had a happy mode.

"Uhhhh…." Good comeback, Cici. That should do it. She's bound to be shaking in her boots now.

"Where is Alex?" she asks casually, which means she doesn't know. "I'm very surprised that he hasn't found you, considering how obvious your collection of companions is in the hallway."

"Uhhhh…." That one probably is the best reply, actually. Though I do swallow at the end, which might have been a giveaway.

Her head twists. "He found you, didn't he?" Yep, it was a giveaway. "Where is he? What happened to him?"

My eyes dart past her to the zombies wandering casually behind her. Her eyes follow—and then get larger.

"Are you telling me that you let those monsters attack him?" She's gone from unhappy to something a little past that fairly quickly.

She's unbuttoning her jacket. Why is she unbuttoning her jacket? Oh, and now she's taking it off. I don't like this.

"What are you doing?" I ask with a slight tremor in my voice.

Carefully and casually she begins to fold her jacket. "I'm sorry, but there are certain transgressions that, well, I just can't let pass."

"You're going to beat the crap out of me," I whisper.

Her smile comes back, and she rises up a little. "Are you asking me if that's my intention, or telling me what you would prefer?"

Prefer? I'm not sure what else she might have been thinking about.

"You can't hurt me. The, um, the doctors and other people they…they need me to do stuff." Oh God, she's going to hurt me.

"Now I'm not sure if you're telling me that I'm incapable of hurting you, or that it's something I shouldn't do," she chirps far too pleasantly.

"Please don't hurt me." The whimper in my voice should make that clear enough.

"Ms. Cole," she still hasn't tried to step around the table, "the fact that I'm going to hurt you is certain, okay? Now, how much I hurt you is a very different matter. You might just wake up with several bad bruises, a limp, and a headache that won't go away for a day or two." She takes a deep breath and her smile…changes. "Or, you can continue to cry and whimper and hide behind that table, and you'll wake up under a doctor's care. Eventually."

There is a sudden loud pounding in the room, filling it completely. It takes me a moment, but I realize that it's the sound of my heart.

Without so much as a regard to me, Alice turns around and steps to the door. She's gonna close it. I'm going to be locked inside this room with her.

She's going to kill me.

Something inside me snaps. The blood that I was hearing rushing through my ears makes its way to my eyes and the world goes red. Before I have any clue what I'm doing I've run around the table and slammed into her back.

I've never really been in a fight before. Not even in high school. So, I do the only thing that I can think of and grab her hair. Immediately I begin to pound her head—or really, more her face—into the door. Each time it hits there is a loud thud that has worked its way past the more rhythmic sound that was my own heartbeat. My breath is short and desperate, and I'm powered right now by pure adrenaline. For a moment, I think I might even make it out of this.

For a moment.

I'm guessing it was her foot, but something rises up quickly and strikes me directly in the groin—hard—and I go down like so much wheat under a scythe. As I lay on the floor, knees crossed and hand firmly on crotch, I can see her through my tears. Her hand comes up a couple of times, touching either her lip or her nose, it's hard to tell. When it pulls back, though, I do see a tint of red on her fingertip.

"Doctor's care it is," she growls.

As she turns around, I do the only thing that I can: I grab ahold of her leg and bite her on the calf. Apparently it's enough, because she screams out. I don't know if it's pain, frustration, or just a primer for what she plans to do, but I'm still going to take it as a minor victory. Best of all, though, is the fact that she stumbles and falls down towards the examination table holding Curly. Not at the right angle so that she hits it, but just enough that as her fall finishes, she's up against it.

A swift kick from her free leg completely dislodges me, not to mention creating one of those bruises that she was mentioning earlier, I'm sure. I skitter away, finding my back against the door she just closed—with the help of me bashing her face into it.

"Ms. Cole, I'm beginning to find myself on the verge of doing something rash." Okay, now I really think she's going to kill me. "If I weren't under contract, I would find every manner of new and interesting levels of pain for you to describe to me."

Her hands move up under her, and I realize she's about to stand up. This is bad.

"Instead, I'm going to use you as an example of why people shouldn't be allowed to plaaaaaahhhhHHHHH!"

The scream was not expected. Then I see why. As she was standing, her ponytail fell right into Curly's hand, and being the decent sort of corpse that he is, he grabbed ahold of it with all his might.

I scramble to my feet and fumble at the door, waiting for the moment that she grabs me.

"Let go! Dammit, let go of me!" she yells behind me, and it's far enough behind me that I open the door completely. The large hallway, filled with zombies whom I'm hoping will all rush to my aid are in front of me…but if I go out there, she still might kill me. I might never get a chance to be rid of her except for right now.

Then I hear the table skid and a faint sound of something like hair tearing as she forces herself to stand up, and I have no idea why I thought any of that. I sprint out into the hallway, desperately hoping that I'll be free and clear.

The sound of her footsteps seems cacophonous behind me, but it is easily drowned out by the ringing sound of metal impacting something solid. I spin around just in time to see her stagger back two or three steps, pursued by Mike and the fire extinguisher in his hands—and suddenly that metallic impact sound makes sense. Doubly so when I see him drive the butt end of it into her face.

Alice collapses on the ground and doesn't move. When she comes to she's probably not going to like the current angle of her nose, I'm guessing. And really, I don't care. I see Mike standing there holding his impromptu weapon, then my eyes move right and I find Julie and Terry nearby.

"Oh God! It's you!"

Terry opens his arms wide as I rush over. He seems a little surprised when I move past him and give Julie a huge hug, though.

"Are you okay?" she asks quickly.

"Yeah. Yeah, I'm scared, but okay." I pull back and get a better look at her. "Are you okay? They didn't hurt you, did they?"

"No, I'm fine. We're fine. They actually took good care of us, even if we were basically in prison," she answers, looking me over as well.

"You're welcome," Terry mumbles.

I turn to look at him, and probably because of all the emotion running through me right now, I smile. "Thanks."

His face lightens up a little. "You're welcome," he says with a touch more sincerity.

"We can't stay here." Mike steps up to us. "This place is chaos right now, but they'll get it together quick enough."

"Okay. Okay, yeah, but we've still gotta get him." I nod through the door at Curly, casually noticing the clump of blond hair in his hand.

"That?" Mike practically recoils at the suggestion. "The zombie, you mean?"

"Yeah. Curly." I look at Terry. "You remember Curly, don't you?"

"Only by reputation," he answers. "I expected him to look better than that."

"Well, we've got to get him up. And fix him up," I explain.

"How?" Mike asks.

"I...I don't know. Maybe... Oh! Grab her jacket," I point to it on the table beside him, "put it on him and then tie it shut with wire. After you stuff all his guts back in, I mean."

"That's disgusting," Julie mutters.

"I can't leave him, Jules. It's my fault he's here." One look at my face and her expression changes.

"You heard her," she says. "Get him put back together and into that jacket!"

"Great! You guys take care of that. I've got one more thing to do." I turn and start to run off, but it's a short run as someone grabs my arm tightly.

"What are you doing?" Terry asks emphatically.

"Just fix this, okay?" I answer.

"I'm not letting you go alone. I'm going with you. They can take care of this." He means it, too.

"No. You've got to stay with Julie and Mike. They don't know how to get out of this place. They need you." I look over at Julie who is still pushing Mike inside the room to take care of Curly.

"But…but where are you going?" Terry asks.

"There's still one prisoner left." I smile. "Don't worry. I'll see you guys outside. Get going."

He hesitates, and I don't blame him. Still, I feel his grip on my arm relax, and with a gentle touch of my other hand I pull my arm free. Before he or anyone else knows what to do, I rush down the hallway with a gang of zombies following close behind.

Chapter Twenty-Eight

I would be totally lost without Didi. Quite literally, I mean. I would be lost wandering these halls if Didi didn't give me not only the tour that she gave, but then directions as to where I needed to go so that I could finally do this one last task before I'm done.

It would really be great to thank her for everything that she's done, but I know that I'm never going to have another conversation with her. After all, she's going to be the one who gets to positively identify my body.

Still, here I am. One last door to deal with and then I'm out. Well, that's the theory, anyway. You never actually know until you do it.

My stolen keycard passes over the lock and it clicks, letting me turn the handle and swing the door inside. I guess the locks are back online.

I'm not sure what I was expecting, but I have to admit that I'm a little disappointed to find a basic office. Just a large desk with a bunch of bookshelves lining the walls. A little larger than normal, giving him plenty of room to walk around, which, from what I find, is something that he is prone to do.

"Dr. Zacek," I say with a nod as I quietly close the door behind me.

His eyes aren't nearly as wide as I would have expected. "Hello, Ms. Cole. I suppose that this was inevitable."

"What? Us having this conversation?"

"No. Well, yes, I suppose, but I was referring to the fact that you're here to kill me."

Now it's my turn for my eyes to bug out, and I'm sure they do it to a rather impressive degree. "What? What the hell are you talking about?"

He stammers a good bit before he actually gives me a reply. "You…aren't here to kill me?"

"No! What kind of person do you think I am?" I shake my head sharply. "No. No killing. I'm very much against killing."

Slowly he walks over to his desk and leans back against it, staring at me the whole time. "Then why are you here? Why aren't you using the chaos to escape?"

"Well, because I'm here to get you, too." I point over my shoulder. "So we can both get out of this place."

"I beg your pardon?" One of his eyebrows goes up. "Are you saying that you're here to rescue me?"

My head bobs around in one of those basically affirmative motions. "Yeah, I guess you could say that."

He stares at me blankly for a full five seconds. "Why?"

That's a question I suppose. Not one I was expecting, but still rather valid. "You told me that you were a prisoner here, too. I'm not going to leave you behind."

"I'm sorry, but I got the distinct impression that you were less than happy to be dealing with me as of late," he half chuckles.

"No, I wasn't. In fact, there were several points there that I wanted to alternately break your kneecaps and bash your skull into my kneecaps, but that's my problem, not yours. Once we're outside you're on your own, but we've got to get you to that point first."

He looks at me and gives a light, pleasant response. "No."

"Are you kidding me?" I blurt out those words before I really have a chance to think about them. "Doc, this is your chance. It's time for us to get out of here."

"No, Ms. Cole. There is no reason to leave. No point to it. We're not going to find success if we leave this place." His reply is so casual and decisive that I can scarcely believe it. "This is the way things are now, and this is how they are going to be."

My jaw drops open. I have no idea how long I stand there staring at him leaning against his desk, but eventually I say the only thing that I can think of.

"Plexiglass."

He blinks a couple of times. "I beg your pardon?"

"Plexiglass," I repeat and take a step towards him. "When we met, you told me that I would be able to figure out what it was that made that waterfall work. Well, lately I've had a lot of time to think about it, and I figured it out. It's plexiglass, isn't it?" My hands start to gesture-construct the image that I see in my mind. "Somehow they got a thick enough piece of plexiglass to stand up on edge, with holes drilled all the way from the base to the top, allowing water to get pumped up through it. Once the water was on the top it flowed over the side and looked to be pouring down from nowhere because the plexiglass disappeared in the water." I take a short breath. "I'm right, aren't I?"

His smile tells me everything that I need to know. "I always said you were clever."

"That's...okay, thanks," I answer, "but that's not the point. The point is that we sometimes don't see what's in front of us because we've already convinced our own mind that reality only works one certain way. That's why the plexiglass trick works. We see the water falling without looking at what's under it. That's not what's important. Water is falling down, so it must be coming from higher up."

He nods slowly. "True, but not relevant here."

"Of course it is!" My arms flail around and I start pacing around myself. "You've convinced yourself that this is reality. That the only way that you'll be able to do what you do—the research that you've been doing—is here in this building. Dammit, there is a whole world outside of this box!"

He laughs lightly again. "And how exactly am I supposed to do anything out there? All of the resources are here. They know what I need and have all the money to give me those things."

Unbelievable. I've had conversations with this guy, so I know that he's not stupid, but at this moment I just want to scream at him. He's blinded himself.

"You don't get it, do you?" I sigh. "It's not the world that you grew up with. Everything has changed. Right now it's kind of scary, too, but that might only be because we don't understand it yet."

"How can you be sure of that?" he counters.

"I can't!" I finally do raise my voice, but immediately lower it back down. "The thing is, I don't want to be in here. I have no desire to stay in this building—or whatever other building might be just like it in another place—and do what I'm told." I move over to stand directly in front of him. "Once I step foot outside this building I'm free to do what I want, and I'll be damned if I'm going to turn around and look backwards wondering what's going on behind me."

"Oh, I'll tell you what will happen. They'll hunt you. They'll discredit you and your friends. They'll do everything that they can to destroy you or to pull you back here and put you under their control once more." He says those words with practiced ease, like a phrase that he's heard in his mind a thousand times before.

"Maybe," I answer, "but how is that going to stop me from trying?" I smile over at him.

"You're being foolish, Cici. This will only backfire on you and make you look bad in their eyes." That tone I'm hearing might even be concern in his voice.

"True, but what you don't understand is that I don't really care. If I end up back here I'm going to have to make them happy again, which might take some time, but if I do end up back here it's because they really wanted me, so what do I really have to lose?"

"You're making a mistake," he says softly. "This is a bad decision."

"Yes! Maybe. I don't know, but I've done a pretty good job of making bad decisions for a while now. I chose a boyfriend who betrayed me. I took a job at a company run by a bunch of evil people. I agreed to help them try to find out if I could relate to zombies. And, ultimately, I gave a zombie a box of cereal. Bad decisions are pretty much my life, Doc," I explain. "But the thing is…they're my decisions. I own them. I made them. It's brought me to where I am today in life, so I can't really be mad at them."

"Don't do this."

"Doc, it's already done. The zombies are already wandering the world. People have seen them and interacted with them. It's not like that's going to go away now," I tell him.

"We're trying to fix that," he replies.

I shake my head. "No, you aren't. You're just trying to get them under your control. The zombies are still going to exist, and I think at this point you guys are just too blind to see that you won't ever be able to bring them back to where you want them. They aren't going to go away."

There is short snort of a laugh before he answers. "I think that you are underestimating what we are capable of doing. With you, we were definitely on the right path."

"No, you weren't." This conversation is over, but for some reason I can't let go just yet. "I was never controlling any zombies, Doc. They were just accepting me as one of their own. They trusted me."

"That's ridiculous!" His face twists up. "Zombies are mindless beasts. Monsters that threaten everything."

"Really? You forget that I worked the front line for a while. They never attacked. In fact, the only stories I ever heard about zombies fighting anyone was when they were defending themselves, and wouldn't you do that, too? Zombies are just a type of life that we don't really understand yet. It's fear and ignorance that causes us to call them monsters."

He simply stares at me. I'm not sure if he's wanting to formulate a response and argue, or if he just feels pity for me. "You can't do this, Ms. Cole. It won't work."

"We'll see. I'm willing to take that chance," I laugh. "What I need to know at this point is where you, personally, stand on things. What are you going to say about me?"

"Me?" His hand comes up to his chest. "I have no part in this matter."

"Good. That means you won't argue about me surviving, then." I might as well tell him.

He doesn't say anything, but his eyes narrow as he tries to take me in more carefully.

"I'm going to die during this escape, Doc," I tell him. "At least, that's what it's going to look like. The zombies are going to turn on me and kill me."

"You just told me that—" He stops himself in mid-sentence and I watch a realization fall over his face. "You'll fake your death."

"That's the plan." My head tilts to one side briefly. "Of course, I don't expect it to last. Eventually they'll figure out that I'm still out there, but by then I'll be long gone." I look him square in the eye. "Assuming that you don't tell them otherwise."

Since the moment that I stepped into this room there has been a heavy air hanging around, permeating everything. Now, for the first time, I do feel a slight sense of lightness.

"I'm no expert on that sort of thing, Ms. Cole. How could I possibly contradict a report that already has you dead?"

The right side of my mouth curls up sharply. "Thanks, Doc. We might not see things the same way, but…. Well, I don't think you're a horrible person. At least not on purpose."

"I'll try to take that as a compliment," he answer with a laugh.

"Take it however you want." I take a deep breath. "I'm sorry that you're not coming with me."

"Don't worry, you'll be back," he says with a smirk.

Silently I walk over to the exit while dozens of possible responses work their way through my head. The door opens easily in my hand, and I see a couple handfuls of figures shuffling about, waiting on me to come out there and join them.

One last time I turn around to look at Dr. Zacek. "No, I don't think so. I've got a lot of others that will be going with me, and I don't think there's going to be space here for all of us." I lower my head slightly. "But just to let you know, we'll always have room for you to come join."

He shakes his head. "Good-bye, Ms. Cole. And, for what it's worth, good luck."

"Well, I can definitely use the luck. You take care of yourself, Doc. I can't say that I understand, but I'm not going to take you with me kicking and screaming." I nod one last time. "Good-bye."

I don't even bother closing the door behind me. Immediately I start down the hall, surrounded by the zombies that have chosen to go with me.

Or maybe I'm choosing to go with them. It's not for me to judge. Either way, we're in this together.

Chapter Twenty-Nine

"You made it."

"Of course she made it! Don't sound so surprised!" I appreciate Julie smacking Mike on the arm for me. It would have been awkward for me to do it so soon.

"Are you okay?" Terry asks. It's sweet in its own way, I suppose.

My mind goes back to the past few minutes. After I left Dr. Zacek's office the way out was direct, but not really simple. With all of the zombies that I had traveling with me, we had that sore thumb quality that so many people talk about. Inevitably we ran into security, who took one look at the couple-dozen-plus zombies wandering down the hall and acted in order—by getting out of the way. No paycheck is really worth being torn to shreds by the living dead, after all.

I suppose they would have stopped me, too, if I didn't already have some practice being a zombie. Sure, it was only one night, but that's the kind of experience that stays with you for a while. All it took was a minute or two to get my hair disheveled and my clothes in disorder and walking among them works just fine—so long as I didn't run into anyone familiar.

The fact that I'm standing on the outskirts of the facility ground talking right now shows that I'm still just another face in the crowd. Granted, it's the dead crowd, but that still qualifies as a crowd.

"Yeah," I finally answer. "Yeah, I think that I am okay, actually."

"I'm so sorry about all of this, Cici." There is a bit of hang-dog puppy eyes in Terry right now. Good. He deserves to feel that way.

"I'm glad to hear that," I answer honestly.

"I…I suppose I deserve that," he sighs.

"You do, but that's okay. You also deserve my thanks. If it wasn't for you, I'd still be in there." I point over my shoulder to the oppressive building behind me.

He steps towards me, taking ahold of my hands and looking into my eyes. "So, what's next for us, then?"

My blinking easily dislodges his gaze. "Us? Oh, there is no us. That ship sailed away and took the population of the island with it. We aren't anything."

"But I thought…well, I hoped that we could start over." His voice is low and honest. "I wasn't kidding, Cici. I love you."

"I believe you. I really do believe that you think you love me, but…no. No, I'm sorry, but I can't, and I won't, look past what happened. I'll forgive you because of what you did since, but I can't forget," I explain.

"Cici, I risked my life for you! I'm still doing it, actually. Doesn't that matter?"

Okay, this is getting old quickly. "Terry, yes, you helped me. You did amazing things for me and put yourself and your life and, well, everything on the line for me," I shake my head, "but you wouldn't have had to do any of that if you hadn't put me in that situation to begin with."

"What do you mean? I didn't do that!" I can tell he wants to shout, but he's thankfully keeping his voice low. "All those F.O.O.D.Z. people are the ones responsible!"

My head shakes slowly back and forth. "Really? Don't you remember me running into the room in tears, terrified for my life because I discovered who was at the facility? Do you remember what you said to me?"

"Yes! I told you I could explain, and I still can. I—"

"No!" A short word and the palm of my hand stops him cold. "You knew. You already knew what was happening and what they wanted to do and who was there and…and you did nothing. The only time you did anything was when you felt guilty about what happened and you came to save me. Well, you know what? Screw you. I appreciate the help, but from now on I'll save myself, thank you very much."

That hurt him. He doesn't say anything, but I can see it in his eyes. That look stings all the way back to me, but I've been learning to shut away pain like that for a while. One more time won't kill me.

"I hate to break up this romantic reunion," Mike steps over to us, whispering loudly, "but we don't have time for this."

Both Terry and I follow his hand as it points over to the multiple cars and trucks that are pulling up in front of the CZC. At first count I put it at a total of six vehicles, but a second time through makes that seven. And they aren't black. I would have expected them to be black, but they are a variety of colors.

"We can't be here when they get inside," he states.

"We'll have a few minutes," I answer. "Didi will take care of things."

Take care. That's a massive understatement. If she's done what she promised, and there is no reason to think she hasn't, then she's already put together a video that shows me being attacked by the zombies in the testing ground. They attack me and kill me dead. A few minutes later I get up and walk out of the room as a member of the living dead.

I suppose that it's really only a half lie.

So, in the time it will take for them to watch the video and then examine the room, I figure I have at least an hour. Of course, they'll probably be sending people out hunting for the zombies, too, so…yeah, maybe I don't have a lot of time, after all.

"On second thought," I state, "you've got the right idea. Let's get out of here."

Looking around we do appear a motley crew. Terry looks beaten, but he'll get over it. He'll also have a chance to get his life back on track if he wants. I don't know if he'll be back at the CZC, but his experience will help him along in this world just fine. There is a fine notch for his cog to slip in somewhere.

Julie and Mike? Oh, I'm not worried about them at all. Mike has connections and a strong background as a police officer. Even if he gets disavowed with everything that he might tell them about what happened, his friends will have his back. He's that kind of guy. No matter what happens, he'll have people supporting him, which is a remarkable thing, really.

And Julie is the type that I never worry about. Not really. In the time that I've known her, she's been the one who kept things in order. I won't be a bit surprised if she's able to take this experience and turn it around to a positive somehow. Beats the hell out of me what that might be, but that's what makes her Julie and me her friend.

"My car is this way," Terry says as he takes point, moving through the brush towards a small shopping center not that far away. He's also our getaway car. At least until he can get us to someplace where we all feel safe. After that…. I've been thinking about that, actually.

Mike goes next, leading the way for Julie. He's always going to be there for her. That makes me feel better about what I have to do, actually.

And that just leaves me—and my newest friend. I look over at Curly. On the surface it appears that he has no clue what is going on. He's just a mindless drone standing still and staring into the distance. At least that's what most people see, but I know better.

I give him a quick smile. "C'mon, Curly. We've got to go."

With a few gestures I convince him to walk with me, and together we step off the grounds of the CZC.

Chapter Thirty

Most people like to think that they are in a civilized world.
Why wouldn't they? They look around and see everything that
they've come to expect as civilization, from roads to housing to
the local grocery store.

What the majority of folks don't realize is that no matter how
deep into civilization they might think they are, they are never
more than a few minutes away from wild. That just over the
hill they are going to find a small herd of deer, or maybe even
a bear that has wandered into their neighborhood. If they look
hard enough, they'll even notice a coyote rummaging through
their garbage or hear a raccoon crawling in the attic.

Or maybe even a huge gathering of zombies just beyond your
back yard.

There was no way that I was going to be able to stay in
civilization. If I had, I would be an open target, easily picked
off by the people behind the CZC, whomever they might be,
and I would probably already be back in a cell. Hell, they still
might be searching for me, but it's a lot tougher to spot a single
person away from the world these days.

Julie and Mike did stay, just like I thought they would. I might have been able to stay with them, but there was no way that I was going to put them at risk. Maybe I could have tried to convince others what happened to me by going public so that if I had disappeared it would have been noticed, making it less likely, but someone would have had to believe me in the first place. My limited experience in that field tells me that all my warnings would have gone unheeded.

On the other hand, Julie has been doing her best to be vocal— not that it is any surprise to me. In fact, she's taken up a rather unusual cause: zombie rights. Yeah, that's right, she's lobbying for zombies to be given certain rights as unique creatures. She's even managed to convert a few to her cause, including my old co-worker Dave from the F.O.O.D.Z. feeding facility. That's going to be one hell of a fight, but I sure wouldn't bet against her.

As for Terry, I couldn't say. The last time I saw him he was driving away after dropping the group of us off at one of Mike's friend's house. I could tell that he wanted to talk to me more, but there was no point. That chapter of my life is over.

For myself, I just think of my new life as an extended camping trip. Strangely enough, I've always hated camping, but it's amazing how well you can adjust to new things when you put your mind to it. And I do have some supplies. Mike is able to sneak some things out to me from time to time. I've got a tent and sleeping bag, and a bit of medicine should the need arise. One of the big items I got from him was duct tape. Don't laugh, that stuff is useful. I've found more that I can do with it than I ever thought possible.

He was a little worried about my safety, and at first so was I, but I quickly came to realize that I had the best security in the world around me. Just a glance around me now and I see

Johnny, Sid, Siouxsie, Patti, Dee Dee, Joey, Tommy, Cheri, Lita, Joan, Lou, Joe, Mick…well, there's a lot of them. And I'm grateful for every single one. I don't think I'd be here without them, actually.

Yeah, I've named every single zombie around me. Sue me. They deserve it.

Oh, and let's not forget Curly. I think he helps me keep this motley band together, actually. I'm not going to bother to wonder why he does it, I'm just going to go on letting him. In return I give him a little help myself. He's much more durable with the duct tape surrounding his torso, and Mike brought out a bicycle helmet to protect his head, to boot.

I suppose the big question is how long can I live out here like this? I don't know. I guess I won't know until I find out, which will either be when I fail or when I finally realize that I don't ever have to go back. I have to fight to stay alive, but that fight makes me feel more alive than I ever have before. Maybe I will return to the norm at some point, but I'd like to think it was because I chose to rather than because I was forced back. Right now, I'm free. Free in a way that I never thought or imagined I would be, and I like it.

As to where I am, well, like I said earlier, you'd be surprised how close the wilds really are to what you consider a tamed place. Which is fine by me. My friends here still need to eat, and I go right up there with them, getting my own bit of food at the same time. I'm one of them now, after all. The first living zombie—at least as far as I know.

So, that's my story. Feeding zombies up to the point where I virtually become one. It's the type of thing that could happen to anyone, really, but this time it happened to me. I'm not complaining. I actually like where I'm at right now, but it's not where I pictured myself being at this point in my life. Not what anyone charted for me at any point. And, for a change, I'm really interested to see what happens next.

Well, not the immediate next. I know what that's going to be. It's just after dawn and my friends are starting to get a bit anxious. A quick look to Curly and a nod in his direction gets things started. Then I just stand up and start shuffling along with everyone else.

"Okay guys," my voice is clear in the morning light, "let's go get something to eat."

My name is Cassandra Cole, and this is my life, such as it is.

It's not that bad, actually.

THE END